CHAPTER ONE

"Try to relax."

"I've never done this before."

Jennifer Cole took a sip from the glass of wine and grimaced. It tasted corked.

"Lean back a bit."

The painter's head tilted as if to get a different perspective on the subject sitting on the chair.

"Let me worry about the hard stuff. You have to look as natural as possible for this to work. Remember what we talked about?"

Jennifer had done this on a whim. She'd seen the advert somewhere – she can't recall where, and she'd sent a message to the number at the bottom. The painter had replied immediately. The portrait would be done at a place of Jennifer's choosing, and if she wasn't satisfied with the finished product, she was under no obligation to pay. It seemed like a win – win situation.

Or perhaps it really was too good to be true.

"That's good."

The painter ran the brush over the canvass and studied Jennifer's face.

"Better."

Jennifer was starting to feel more at ease. The wine seemed to have helped. The painter said it would. She took another, longer drink and closed her eyes.

"She opened them a moment later. "Sorry."

"It's OK. I've already got what I need. Close them again – I like it."

"How long have you been doing this?" Jennifer asked.

Her voice sounded alien in her ears. Her senses were playing tricks on her and it was as though the voice was no longer her own.

"You're my first. We're nearly done. You really are an exceptional subject."

"This wine tastes funny," Jennifer said, but took another sip anyway.

"It's Bulgarian."

Jennifer giggled at this without knowing why.

"Can I see what you've done so far?" she asked.

"Soon."

"I'm going to give the portrait to my girlfriend," Jennifer said, and giggled again. "It's her birthday next week."

"A thoughtful gift. Your soul is captured on this canvas. It's everlasting – it will be here long after you've gone."

Jennifer was feeling very drunk now. Her limbs were weak, and she could sense that her heartbeat was slowing.

"I don't feel well," she managed to say.

"No, I don't imagine you do."

Jennifer couldn't hold onto the wine glass anymore. It slipped from her hand and landed with a dull thud on the carpet.

"What have you..."

"Shh."

The painter was standing over her now. Jennifer Cole was conscious of something being placed in her lap but that was the last thing her senses picked up. She felt nothing as the razor blade carved an arc in her neck and she wasn't aware of the painter adding the final touches to the portrait with some of the blood that had gushed from her arteries.

"I'm so, so sorry."

Jennifer couldn't hear this. Nor did she feel the gentle touch of the painter's lips as they placed a kiss on the top of her head.

CHAPTER TWO

"You've mixed up the paints again."
Laura Smith gave her adopted sister Lucy a look only an eight-year-old can pull off. The two girls were making a start on a new painting-by-numbers project. It had become something of an obsession for them during the lockdowns. The restrictions had now been lifted and soon life was supposed to get back to normal - Lucy and Laura were free to go out whenever they chose, but the lure of the painting-by-numbers always seemed to win.

The latest painting was of a tiger in the jungle. Lucy had indeed mixed up the paints, and Laura had realised as soon as she'd started on the stripes of the great cat. The greens and blues on its fur were definitely not what a tiger should look like to her.
"It makes it more interesting," Lucy insisted. "Anyone can paint a tiger that looks like a tiger."
"That makes no sense whatsoever," Laura said. "You're weird. Something broke in your brain when you had Andrew."

Right on cue, the wails of a baby could be heard. Lucy had given birth to the boy last year. Andrew Jason Smith had recently celebrated his first birthday - it was clear he'd woken up and if he didn't get some food soon, he would let them know all about it.
"I'll go," Laura offered.
"Are you sure?" Lucy said. "He'll probably need a change."
"I have done it before."
"Darren can do it."
"I'll go," Laura said. "This painting is all wrong anyway."

She got up and left the room. Darren Lewis came in shortly afterwards. Darren was Andrew's father. The seventeen-year-old had moved into the

Smith household shortly before the first lockdown and he wasn't showing any signs of moving out anytime soon.

He glanced at the painting. "Don't you get bored of them?"

"It's relaxing," Lucy said.

"We are allowed to leave the house now," Darren reminded her. "It's summer – we should be out having fun."

"I like painting. It helps me to take my mind off things."

"We can take Andy down to the park," Darren said.

"Will you stop calling him that."

"It's his name."

"His name is Andrew," Lucy said.

"He's going to be called Andy by all of his mates. Get used to it."

"His name is Andrew," Lucy said once more.

"What time will your parents be home?" Darren changed the subject very blatantly.

"They should be back at around five. Office hours. The lockdowns made it difficult for people to go out and commit crime, and it seems like the crime lull has carried on. My dad is going crazy."

"Your dad is not right in the head," Darren said. "Would he prefer it if people started killing each other again?"

"Yes," Lucy replied without thinking. "He would."

* * *

Detective Sergeant Jason Smith was bored stiff. He was smoking his second cigarette in quick succession outside the station. He had absolutely nothing to do. The last year or so had passed by agonisingly slowly, and even the distraction of a new baby in the house hadn't helped. There hadn't been a single murder in York since the first lockdown was announced – the *Loner* investigation was a distant memory now, and Smith longed for a juicy case to sink his teeth into.

He'd just lit a third cigarette when DS Whitton came outside.

"Has something happened?" Smith asked his wife.

"What do you think?" she said.

"I'm going to end up in a loony bin if people don't start committing murder soon."

"Be careful what you wish for," Whitton said.

"I'm always careful what I wish for, and what I want more than anything right now is for the coldblooded killers of this city to show their faces again."

"You don't mean that."

"I do mean it," Smith said. "It's what I do, Erica. It's what we both do."

Whitton's phone beeped to tell her she'd received a message. She swiped the screen and smiled.

She showed the photograph to Smith. "He's growing up so quickly."

Smith smiled too. The photo was of Andrew. Sandwiched between two dogs the year-old baby seemed perfectly content to have the combined weight of a portly Bull Terrier and a grotesque Pug on top of him. Theakston and Fred had taken to the baby from the start and both of them took their guard duties very seriously.

"We need to talk about Darren," Smith said out of the blue. "The lockdown is over, so there's no reason why he has to live with us anymore."

"I thought you'd got used to it," Whitton said. "It was your idea, remember."

"It was a practical solution to the situation at the time. That situation has changed."

"Lucy likes having him around. He helps out a lot with Andrew."

"He can't live with us forever," Smith said. "We don't have the room."

"He's seventeen, Jason. What he makes from his IT work isn't enough for him to rent a place, and he'll be going back to college in September."

"He can go back to his parents' house. I'm just saying that this arrangement was never meant to be permanent."

He stubbed out his cigarette and, after staring at the packet for a moment he decided not to smoke another one.

"What are we actually doing here?" he asked.

"We're paid to be here," Whitton said.

"It feels like this past year has been something from a film script. And not a very good script at that. 2020 was basically a write-off – a non-year if that makes any sense."

"It's been tough for everyone," Whitton said. "You're starting to whine a lot in your old age."

"I'll be forty next year. That's more than halfway to death according to statistics. It's actually quite depressing when you think about it."

Whitton looked at her watch. "It's almost time to knock off."

"Another *Groundhog Day* clocked up then."

Whitton was glad when PC Baldwin came outside. She'd heard enough of Smith's maudlin ramblings.

"We've had a report of a body."

Smith was wide awake. "A murder?"

"Definitely. A woman came home and found her girlfriend dead. Her throat has been slashed open."

"It looks like your wish has been granted," Whitton said.

"About time," Smith said.

"Grant Webber is already there," Baldwin said.

"What's the address?" Smith asked.

Baldwin told them, and Smith and Whitton headed for Whitton's car. The smile on Smith's face was rather inappropriate given the circumstances, but Smith didn't care.

CHAPTER THREE

The dead woman lived in Murton. Number 45 Highfield Avenue was a stone's throw from the local Sainsbury's, and that's where Whitton was forced to park. The road was jampacked with vehicles. Two police cars were parked opposite number 45. An ambulance was in position behind them, and Grant Webber's vehicle was also on the scene. Even though it had been a long time since he'd had to attend the scene of a murder, the Head of Forensics clearly hadn't lost his touch. As long as Smith had known him, Webber had always arrived at the scene before anybody else.

Smith and Whitton got out of the car.
"Remind me to pick up some beer from the Sainsbury's when we're finished," Smith said.
"We're supposed to be working," Whitton said.
"And we're parked in the car park of a supermarket. It would be rude not to buy something while we're here. Besides, I'm running low on beer."
"You and your beer."
"Beer is the answer to all life's problems, my dear. Let's go and see what we're dealing with, shall we?"

He spotted DI Oliver Smyth next to one of the police cars and walked over to him.
"Afternoon, boss," Smith said. "What do we know?"
"Webber and Billie are inside now," DI Smyth said. "Early indications are the woman was killed where she was found – in the living room. Single wound to the throat. She would have bled out in minutes."
"Who found her?"
"Girlfriend. She's next door with the neighbour. I've organised a door-to-door, but until we've spoken to the girlfriend, we won't have much of a

timeline to go on."

"What do we know about the victim?" Smith asked.

He took out his cigarettes and lit one.

DI Smyth's facial expression told him he wasn't impressed.

"It helps me to think," Smith explained.

"All we know at this point is what I've already told you."

Smith looked up and down the road. Highfield Avenue was a typical mid-twentieth century housing development with semi-detached properties on both sides of the road. It was late Thursday afternoon and the cars parked in most of the driveways told him that most of the residents had returned home from work.

"What are you looking for?" DI Smyth asked him.

"CCTV," Smith replied. "More and more people feel the need to put up cameras these days. It's totally at odds with their gripes about personal privacy. That one looks promising."

He pointed to the house directly opposite number 45. Two cameras were clearly visible, one on either side of the property.

"The camera on the left is pointing straight at the front of number 45."

"The officers doing the door-to-doors will ask about any cameras," DI Smyth said.

"Someone has just come out," Smith said. "I'm going to speak to him. Webber won't let me anywhere near the scene yet anyway."

He threw his cigarette butt down and crossed the road.

The man standing in the doorway looked to be in his thirties. He was dressed in a T-shirt and a pair of shorts. Smith walked up to him and explained who he was. The man didn't invite him in.

"Can I have your name please?" Smith said.

"What for?"

"When a police officer asks you for your name, you're supposed to give it."

"Bernard," the man said with a shrug of the shoulders. "Bernard Ford. What's going on?"

"I don't know yet," Smith said. "I couldn't help noticing your CCTV cameras."

"They're not against the law."

"I didn't say they were. I'd like to take a look at the footage if that's alright."

"They're not switched on," Bernard said.

"What's the point of having them if they're not switched on?" Smith asked.

"Ask the dykes across the road."

"I'm not following you."

Bernard pointed directly at number 45. "Those lesbos thought I put up the cameras so I could perv on them."

"Lesbos?" Smith said.

"Lesbians," Bernard said. "Muff bandits, whatever you want to call them. They seemed to think I installed the cameras so I could spy on them. Bloody dykes."

Smith suddenly wondered what century he was living in. He didn't think people like Bernard Ford existed anymore.

"What has your cameras being turned off got to do with the women who live across the road?" he asked.

"They got a court order telling me I wasn't allowed to have the cameras pointing at them."

"Why didn't you just move them?" Smith said. "Aim them towards the ground? Surely you don't need to see all the way across the road."

"I couldn't be bothered. It was easier just to switch them off. Their sort have all the rights these days, don't they? Normal blokes like us are fighting a losing battle, aren't we?"

Smith didn't comment on this.

"So, the cameras are definitely not recording?" he said instead.

"Are you saying you don't believe me?"

"I assume you live alone," Smith said.

"Is it that obvious?"

It certainly is, Smith thought.

Bernard Ford was starting to get on his nerves.

"Someone will be around shortly to speak to you," he said.

"What for? What exactly happened across the road?"

"I don't know. Like I said, someone will come and talk to you."

He turned around and crossed back over the road.

"Anything?" DI Smyth asked.

"The piece of human waste I spoke to reckons his cameras are switched off," Smith said.

"You didn't make a new friend there then?"

"I doubt that bigoted moron has any friends. I want to take a look inside number 45."

"All in good time," DI Smyth said. "Webber has been in there for quite a while, so I get the feeling it's not a simple one."

A red Subaru BRZ pulled up and managed to squeeze into the space between the ambulance and one of the police cars. DS Bridge and DC Moore got out and joined Smith and DI Smyth. Bridge stretched his arms and Smith heard something click in his back.

"Next time we're taking my car," Bridge said to DC Moore.

"Your Toyota can't go more than fifty miles per hour," the man from London said.

"My car doesn't cause spinal trauma every time I get into it," Bridge said. "That thing of yours is ridiculous."

"What have we got?" DC Moore asked.

"Dead female," DI Smyth said. "Her name is Jennifer Cole. The girlfriend came home and found her. Webber and Billie are in there now."

Bridge's eyes lit up. "Do we know anything else?"

"It looks like her throat was cut. That's about all we've got so far. We'll know more when we've spoken to the girlfriend."

"I'll know more when I'm allowed to have a look inside the house," Smith added.

"What's wrong with you?" DI Smyth said.

"What's wrong with me? It's been so long since I've attended a murder scene, I've forgotten what one looks like, and right now, I'm standing around like a lost fart a stone's throw away from a dead woman. I need to take a look."

"Here's Webber now," Bridge said.

Smith was on him in a shot. The Head of Forensics smiled and shook his head.

"Don't," he said. "I know exactly what you're going to say. I'll get you a suit, and you can go and take a look for yourself."

"I've missed you, Webber," Smith said.

"I can't say I feel the same," Webber said and looked him up and down. "The suit might be a bit tight – you've put on a good few pounds during lockdown."

CHAPTER FOUR

Billie Jones was taking photographs of something in the hallway when Smith went inside number 45 Highfield Avenue. She nodded to Smith and carried on snapping away. He didn't ask her what she was so interested in – he needed to see the scene of the first murder in over a year. He'd been told that the dead woman was in the living room and when he reached the door to the room he stopped. The air inside the house was thick with a peculiar stench. Smith recognised the metallic tang of blood – he was very familiar with that smell, but what caught his attention now was another, more pungent odour. It crept inside his nostrils and burned his throat as he breathed it in.

"What is that smell?" he asked Billie.
"You'll understand when you see what's in there," she said and turned her attention back to something on the table in the hallway.

Smith stepped inside the living room and emptied his head of all thoughts not connected with what he was doing right now. He needed to disconnect himself from everything else.

Jennifer Cole was sitting on a single seater chair in front of the fireplace. Smith sensed immediately that this wasn't where the chair usually was. It had been moved into this position. Above the fireplace was an intricate painting of something Smith couldn't quite figure out. He guessed it was supposed to be modern art. The entire canvas was taken up with Roman numerals pieced together randomly. Some of them were upside down. Smith wasn't a big fan of art, but he had to admit there was a strange kind of aesthetic appeal to this piece.

He turned his attention to the woman on the chair. She looked to be in her late-twenties, early-thirties with short blonde hair. Her chin was resting on the top of her chest and her unblinking eyes were staring downwards.

The T shirt she was wearing was soaked with blood. Some of that blood had made its way onto the object on her lap. Smith crouched down and took in the painting. It was a portrait – that was very clear, and Smith studied it carefully. It was obvious the artist who had painted it was very talented. Jennifer's face had been recreated beautifully. Smith noticed that the fireplace and the modern piece of art above it were also in the painting.

"What do you think?" Grant Webber asked from behind.
Smith turned around. "Did you find the paints?"
Webber shook his head. "Nothing. Looks like he took them with him."
"This was painted very recently, wasn't it? You can still smell it."
"Some of the canvas is still wet," Webber said. "And it looks like he used her blood for parts of it."
Smith looked directly at him. "Are you alright?"
"It was a long time ago. What else can you see?"
"The artist is very good. He's captured her face well, and the details of the fireplace and the artwork above it are really intricate. This must have taken quite a while. Do we know if she was alive when the painting was done?"
"We don't know much at the moment," Webber said. "We'll make the painting a priority. It'll be easy to tell if she was added on afterwards."

Smith looked at the artwork on the wall and then he focused his attention on the portrait of the dead woman.
"He's managed to capture the Roman numerals in great detail. Why bother doing that if he planned on leaving the painting here with the victim?"
"Perhaps he's a perfectionist. Who knows. There was a wine glass on the carpet, and we found an empty bottle in the kitchen. They've been bagged and we'll be examining them too."
"Do you suspect that she might have been drugged first?" Smith asked.
"I believe she was. The wound on her neck is clean – ear-to-ear, and that's hard to pull off if your victim is able to put up a fight. Have you seen

enough?"

Smith's eyes narrowed, and he moved closer to the painting.

"I don't know what to make of this."

"What are you thinking?" Webber asked.

"Was there any sign of forced entry?"

"Nothing. No broken windows or damaged locks."

"She let him in," Smith decided. "There's nothing inside this room to suggest a struggle took place. I think she knew her killer."

"Let's not get ahead of ourselves."

"It's how I operate," Smith reminded him. "I get ahead of myself then take a step back when I decide I've gone too far. My first impressions of this scene are she knew her killer. She felt comfortable with him. She allowed him to paint her, and that will have taken quite some time. She was definitely drugged – there was something in that wine that rendered her unconscious. But there's one thing that strikes me as *off* about the whole scene."

"Go on."

"Why leave the portrait behind?" Smith said. "What purpose does that serve? Surely if he's gone to all this trouble, he will want something to take away from it."

"I still have a lot to get through," Webber said. "And your speculations are slowing me down."

Smith took out his phone and took a few photographs of the painting.

He straightened up again, took another look around the room and gave Webber a pat on the back.

"I'm fine," the Head of Forensics said. "Really."

"I'll leave you to it," Smith said. "This suit is starting to itch."

He went back outside, removed the SOC suit and lit a cigarette. Something about the scene inside the living room of number 45 was bothering him. Why did the person who painted the portrait leave it behind?

As trophies went, Smith couldn't think of a much better one, so why did the killer not take it with him? He walked over to DI Smyth.

"Are you happy now?" DI Smyth asked.

"Not really," Smith said. "There's something very wrong with the scene in there."

He told him about the portrait.

"That is odd," DI Smyth agreed. "If you set out to paint a portrait before killing someone you take the painting with you when you're finished. Perhaps he was interrupted."

"I don't think he was. Forensics didn't find the paints anywhere inside the house, and that portrait was painted recently. Some of the paint is still wet. He also used some of her blood to finish it off. I get the impression he had plenty of time to clear up, so why leave the painting behind?"

"How is Webber handling it?" DI Smyth asked. "This must be bringing back some painful memories."

"He's bearing up, but it has to affect him - looking at the victim must hurt. Has anyone spoken to the girlfriend?"

"Whitton and DC King are with her now. I thought it would be better if a couple of female officers spoke to her."

"I agree," Smith said. "I think she knew her killer, boss. Hopefully Whitton and Kerry can get some clues from the girlfriend."

CHAPTER FIVE

Patti Apple was a tall woman in her late thirties. She had fine features and striking blue eyes. Whitton and DC King were sitting opposite her in the house next door to number 45. The neighbour had graciously left them in peace.

"Mrs Apple," Whitton said. "We really are very sorry about Jennifer."
"Miss," Patti said. "I'm not married – never have been. Call me Patti."
"Patti," Whitton obliged. "I know this isn't easy, but we have to ask you a few questions and we need to do that now."
Patti nodded. "It's alright. Jennifer and I watch a lot of crime series. Time is always of the essence, isn't it? The first forty-eight hours are the most crucial."

"Is there someone we can call for you?" DC King asked. "A relative or a friend perhaps."
"I'll phone my brother later," Patti said.
"How long have you and Jennifer been together?" Whitton said.
She'd made up her mind to refer to her in the present tense for now. In her experience, she knew the relatives of victims tended to be more forthcoming with information this way.

"Six years," Pattie replied. "I met her at a *Slipknot* concert. It was in Manchester and *Korn* were the support act. It was amazing."
"You don't strike me as someone who listens to *Slipknot*," DC King said.
Patti smiled a half smile. "That's what everybody tells me. The music has so much energy in it. My boss frowns when he learns about the concerts Jennifer and I attend."
"What do you do for a living?" Whitton said.
"I'm an accountant."
"What about Jennifer?" DC King said. "What does she do?"

"She's a teaching assistant at a primary school. She loves that job. Her children will be devastated. She always calls them that – *my children*."

"You're doing great," Whitton said. "Can you tell us some more about Jennifer. What about your circle of friends?"

"It's not a very big one," Patti said. "There are a few people we socialise with once in a while, but I'd say they're more acquaintances than friends. Do you think someone we know did this to her?"

"It's more common than you think," DC King said.

"It's always the husband, isn't it? Isn't that always the first thing the police look into?"

"Unfortunately, it does happen," Whitton said. "When did you last see Jennifer?"

"This morning when I left for work. The school holidays have just started so Jennifer didn't have to go to work, but she always gets up early anyway. I've been working from home a lot, but now things seem to have returned to normal I go into the office more often."

"What time was this?" DC King said.

"I usually leave at around eight."

"And Jennifer was up?" Whitton said.

"She was. The schools won't be open again until September, but she still has a lot of work to do in preparation. The children have a lot of catching up to do."

"You left for work at eight," Whitton said. "What time did you return home?"

"Five minutes before I phoned you," Patti said. "I went inside the house, and…"

"It's alright," DC King said.

"Oh my God…"

Patti shot to her feet and raced out of the room.

She came back a few minutes later. Her eyes were very bloodshot now and there were spots of vomit on her shirt.

"I'm sorry," she said. "That came from nowhere."

"It's OK," DC King said.

"Do you need to go to the hospital?" Whitton asked. "We can arrange for someone to take you there."

"No," Patti said. "It's passed now. I have to get some work done. We have an audit that needs to be submitted before Monday – it's one of our biggest clients."

"Don't worry about that," Whitton told her. "Someone else can take care of it. Can you think of anyone who might have wanted to hurt Jennifer? Did she mention anything about any threats? Did she get the impression that anyone was watching her?"

"No. She didn't say anything like that. Do you think someone has been stalking her?"

"We have to consider all possibilities," Whitton said.

The neighbour came inside the room.

"Is there anything you need?" she asked.

"Could you get Patti a glass of water please?" Whitton said.

"Of course. Would you like something to drink?"

"No thanks."

"I don't know what to do, Kelly," Patti told her neighbour. "What am I going to do without Jennifer?"

"I phoned Pete," Kelly said. "He's tied up with work, but he said he'll get here as soon as he can."

"Pete's my brother," Patti explained.

"I'll get you that water," Kelly said.

"Who would do that to her?" Patti said. "Did you see what they did to her?"

"This might be a difficult question to answer," Whitton said. "But has Jennfer been acting strangely recently? Has she been behaving out of character in any way?"

"Not that I recall."

"And she hasn't received any unusual phone calls?" DC King said. "Calls she hasn't been able to explain to you?"

"No."

"We'll be going through her call log," Whitton said. "And we may need you to help us with that if it's OK."

"I'll help you with anything," Patti said. "I'll assist you with anything that will make sure whoever did this to her rots in hell for the rest of their lives. Why would someone do that? Jennifer has never hurt anyone in her life."

Whitton reached inside her pocket for her card, but when she looked at it, she realised it was an old one of Smith's.
She gave it to Patti. "If you think of anything else, give us a ring. These are Detective Sergeant Smith's details, but he'll be more than happy to take your call."

"Are you going to catch them?" Patti said. "Are you going to find out who did this to Jennifer?"

"We'll find out," Whitton said. "That's a promise. We will not stop until whoever is responsible for this pays for what they've done."

CHAPTER SIX

"Do you realise," Smith said. "This is the first briefing we've had in 2021."
"You're forgetting about the New Year stabbing," DC Moore corrected him.
Smith raised any eyebrow. "That was hardly worth writing home about."
A man had been stabbed outside a nightclub in the early hours of the first day of the new year. He was stabbed in the arm – the wound was superficial, and it had taken them less than twenty-four-hours to wrap it up. His girlfriend had confessed and the victim didn't press charges. Smith thought they were probably still together.

"Let's get moving with what we know," DI Smyth began. "Jennifer Cole was killed in her living room sometime between eight this morning and five this afternoon. Her throat was sliced open, and she was left on display with a portrait of herself in her lap. Any thoughts?"
Smith was the first to voice his opinion.
"She knew her killer."
"The evidence at the scene does seem to suggest this," DI Smyth said. "Forensics found no evidence of forced entry and there was nothing to indicate that any kind of struggle took place."
"It's also looking likely that she was drugged before she was killed," Smith added. "The wound to her neck was clean – a precision cut, and it would be almost impossible to inflict such a wound if the victim was defending themselves. She had no defensive wounds, and that suggests the killer was free to kill her at will."
"There was an empty wine glass on the carpet next to the chair she was sitting on," DI Smyth said. "And a bottle in the kitchen. We'll know by tomorrow, latest if there were any traces of sedative in either."

"What do we know about the victim?" Bridge said.

"She was twenty-nine," Whitton said. "And she worked as a teaching assistant at one of the primary schools in the city."

"She works full time," DC King said. "And now it's the school holidays, so she'll be off until September."

"It's possible our killer knew this," DC Moore said. "He might have known she would be home alone."

"He was definitely aware of her routine," Smith said. "What about the girlfriend? What did you get from her?"

"She was at work when the attack was carried out," Whitton said. "We've spoken to her employers, and they've confirmed it. She arrived at the accountancy firm where she works at half-eight this morning, and she was there all day until she left at half-four."

"A painting was found at the scene," DI Smyth said. "A portrait of Miss Cole, and we have reason to believe it was painted before she was killed."

"Whoever painted it knew what they were doing," Smith said. "That portrait was created by an extremely talented artist, and I believe it would have taken quite some time to paint it."

"Why leave it there?" It was DC King.

"I'm glad we're on the same page, Kerry," Smith said. "Why indeed? You go to all the trouble of painting a portrait and then you leave it behind. Why would you do that?"

"Perhaps he's not a trophy collector," Bridge suggested. "Not all serial killers collect trophies."

"As far as we're aware," DI Smyth said. "This is an isolated incident. There is nothing to indicate that we're dealing with a serial murderer."

Smith nodded and remained silent.

"Harry," DI Smyth said. "Can you do the honours with the screen?"

"No problem, sir," DC Moore said.

He connected the laptop to the huge screen at the back of the room. After tapping the keypad a few times an image appeared on the screen. It was a close-up of the painting that had been left in Jennifer Cole's lap.

"It really is good," DC King said. "Look at the detail in her eyes."

"She was definitely alive when he painted it then," Bridge decided.

Of this there was little doubt. Jennifer Cole was leaning back in the chair, but her eyes were focused directly on the person painting the portrait.

"We still don't have an accurate timeline to look at," DI Smyth said. "We'll have that when we have a time of death, so what we need to do in the meantime is go through the preliminary motions. Who was Jennifer Cole and why did someone want her dead? We'll speak to her family and friends, as well as her work colleagues."

"That portrait is important, boss," Smith said.

"I agree, but we'll do this one step at a time if you don't mind. I appreciate it's been a while since the last murder investigation, but we cannot afford to rush into this at breakneck speed and risk overlooking important information while we're doing that."

"How's Webber bearing up?" Bridge asked.

"He reckons he's OK," Smith said. "But it must be tough for him."

"Why?" DC Moore said.

"He lost someone very close to him in similar circumstances," DI Smyth said. "And that's all I'm going to say on the subject. We have work to do. Smith, you and Kerry can take the school where Jennifer Cole worked."

Smith wasn't listening. His eyes were focused on the image on the screen. Jennifer Cole's brown eyes were staring right at him. There was no indication in them that she was drowsy from whatever drug she'd been given, but Smith decided the artist could have done that intentionally.

His gaze shifted to the intricate piece of modern art in the background. Why had the killer taken the trouble to include this in the painting? Surely it was unnecessary in a portrait, and it served only to take the attention away from the subject of the piece. Smith couldn't understand why the painter had replicated this piece of art. It was more of a distraction than anything else.

"Smith," DI Smyth broke his train of thought. "Are you still with us?"

"Still with you, boss," Smith confirmed.

"You and Kerry can speak to Miss Cole's work colleagues. It's school holidays but you'll be able to get a list of employees from the school. Whitton, you and Bridge can look into her family and friends. I want a better picture of the woman before the end of the day. Harry, you and I are going to take a trip back to Highfield Avenue."

"What for, sir?" DC Moore said.

"Because one of the neighbours mentioned something interesting during the door-to-door, and I want to get some more details from him."

CHAPTER SEVEN

"God, that stinks."

Darren Lewis recoiled from the stench coming from his son's nappy. He'd become a dab hand at changing the baby now, but he was still unprepared for some of the surprises the year-old boy threw his way.

"What did you feed him yesterday?" he added.

"He had the same as usual," Lucy said. "Hold on, no. I mashed up some sweet potato for him. It's really good for him."

"Well it's not good for me. Could you warn me next time."

"It doesn't smell that bad," Lucy said.

She ruffled the baby's hair and kissed him on both cheeks.

"You don't smell, Andrew. Daddy's such a baby sometimes, isn't he?"

Darren cleaned what needed cleaning and wrapped up the nappy. He held it at arm's length as if it might bite him at any time and went to find somewhere to dispose of it. Lucy finished off by rubbing in some cream and putting on a clean nappy.

Darren returned with a concerned look on his face.

"What's wrong?" Lucy said and handed Andrew to him.

"Your dad has been hinting about me moving out."

"My dad doesn't do hints," Lucy said. "If he wanted you out, he would have come right out with it."

"I know what I've heard. He keeps mentioning stuff about the lockdowns being over, and how he hopes everything will get back to normal."

"He was probably talking about work. He's a police detective – he lives for his job, and the past year has been hard on him."

"Perhaps we should look for a place of our own," Darren said. "I don't want to overstay my welcome."

"How?" Lucy said. "We can't afford to pay rent on what you make from your IT jobs. And I'm not looking for a job, if that's what you want."

Lucy had aced her GCSEs despite the pregnancy and the lockdown, and she was halfway through her A levels. She'd completed the majority of the coursework remotely but that had suited her fine. It meant she didn't have to leave Andrew with a friend or family member. Darren was due to start his second year of college in a couple of months too, and a fulltime job would make things complicated there.

"I don't expect you to get a job," he said. "You're the brains of this outfit, and you're going to make use of those brains, but I think if I could get more work, we would be able to afford the rent on a place."

"You're supposed to be going back to college," Lucy reminded him. "I thought that was what you wanted."

"I can do both. Most of my IT jobs can be done from my laptop anyway. I can do it after college."

"No," Lucy decided. "It won't work. We've got Andrew to consider, and he's better off here than in some poky flat."

"Are you sure your dad doesn't want me out?"

"Positive."

"Do you think we're going to be alright?" Darren asked.

"Ask him," Lucy snuggled up to Andrew.

Her hair tickled his face and he giggled with pleasure.

"We've just got through one of the worst years in the history of this country," Lucy said. "I think if we can make it through that we can survive anything. He'll be hungry."

"I'll sort him out," Darren offered. "No sweet potatoes though."

"How is your brother getting on with my dad's car?" Lucy asked at the table in the kitchen.

Andrew was suitably fed, and his drooping eyelids were telling them he was about to nod off in his highchair.

"He reckons the Sierra is past saving," Darren said.

"Mum's been telling Dad that for years."

"Our Gary is a really good mechanic," Darren said. "My dad has taken a look at it too, and he thinks it's time Mr Smith got a new car. I've been too scared to tell him."

"I'll let Mum know. She'll tell him with pleasure. It might be better to make yourself scarce when she does though."

"I will. I'd better put Andy down. He can hardly keep his eyes open."

"His name is Andrew," Lucy said.

Darren smiled at her.

"And that smile doesn't work on me like it used to."

"In your dreams."

Darren scooped up the baby and held him close. He was already fast asleep.

"What was your dad like?" he asked when he came back. "Your real dad I mean."

"Why do you ask?" Lucy said.

"You don't talk about him much."

"No, but I never stop thinking about him. He was an amazing dad. A gentle soul. All he ever wanted out of life was to help people. I think that's why I get on so well with Smith – he and my dad were very much alike."

"I can't see Detective Sergeant Smith as being a gentle soul."

"It runs deeper with Smith. What you see on the surface isn't the real Smith – he's the second kindest person I've ever met. He and Whitton were there for me when my dad was killed and they're still here for me."

"I suppose I'll have to wait for the gentle Smith to show his face when I'm around."

"He will," Lucy said. "Did you know that after my dad was attacked and I asked if I could stay with them, Smith said OK without even thinking about it. And when it was a choice between me going into care or them adopting me, he agreed to that on the spot too. Not many men would do that."

"What do you want to do?" Darren asked. "Andy... Sorry, Andrew is going to be asleep for ages. Do you want to watch something on Netflix?"
"It's not even eleven in the morning. Watching TV during the day is depressing."
"What do you suggest then? We can't go out and leave Andrew on his own."
"Painting by numbers," Lucy said. "Give it a go – it really is addictive after a while."

CHAPTER EIGHT

Derek James lived at number 28 Hatfield Avenue. When uniforms had been carrying out a routine door-to-door Mr James had mentioned seeing something odd yesterday. It had been PC Griffin who'd realised that the retired fireman might have seen something important, and he'd diligently taken a statement from him.

"Thank God for that."

Derek was a stocky man. He was fifty-eight but he looked much younger. He looked to DI Smyth like a man who liked to keep himself in shape.

"Excuse me," DC Moore said.

"I thought they were going to send the pillock from yesterday," Derek said.

"You're referring to PC Griffin?" DI Smyth said.

"I'm referring to the idiot who wasted two hours of my life writing out something that should have taken ten minutes. Where do you recruit them from these days – arsehole college?"

DI Smyth found himself smiling, and he secretly wished Smith was here to hear this.

The PC in question was an objectionable man with ideas far above his station. There was little doubt that PC Griffin was on a fast track to the top – his education and his knowledge of the correct procedure where arse kissing was concerned would make sure of that, but in his short time with York Police he'd already rubbed a lot of his colleagues up the wrong way. Smith and PC Griffin had clashed heads virtually from the onset, and DI Smyth didn't doubt there would be many more altercations to come.

After explaining who they were Derek invited them in. He didn't offer them coffee because he didn't have any.

"Years of knocking back gallons of the stuff when I was a firefighter made me hate the stuff," he explained. "I have tea if you fancy a cup."
DI Smyth declined.
"I wouldn't mind a cuppa," DC Moore said.
"Coming up."

"You said in your statement you noticed something suspicious yesterday," DI Smyth said.
Derek had made DC Moore a cup of tea, but he wasn't having anything himself.
"That's right," Derek said.
"The statement PC Griffin took from you was seven pages long," DC Moore said. "Could you give us the abridged version?"
"It was about noon. I was up in my study working on my book when I caught site of the courier van out of the corner of my eye. I thought it might be a CD I'd ordered, so I went downstairs to wait for it."
"But it wasn't your CD?" DI Smyth said.
"No. I was a bit disappointed. It's a rare copy of Motorhead's *Overkill* album. It's a hard CD to find."
"I remember that from the statement," DC Moore said.
"One of many irrelevant pieces of information that tosser felt the need to include. No offence – I know he's one of your lot."
"None taken," DI Smyth said. "Carry on."
He made a mental note to have a word with PC Griffin about what to and what not to include when taking a statement in the future.

"It wasn't my CD," Derek said. "The van parked down the road outside number 45, or it could have been number 47."
"Why did you think that was unusual?" DC Moore said. "There are a lot of courier vans on the roads these days."

"Because it was there all afternoon."

"Perhaps it belonged to someone who lives on the street," DI Smyth said.

"I've never seen it before."

"Did you get a look at the driver of the van?" DC Moore asked.

"Not really," Derek said. "I didn't really think much of it when it arrived. Like you said, couriers are everywhere these days. The driver got out with something in his hands and walked up to either number 45 or 47. The front doors are pretty much right next to each another."

"What about the van itself?" DI Smyth said. "How could you be so sure it was a courier?"

"Because of the decals on the side. *Harvey's Couriers*."

DC Moore made a note of it.

"What colour was the van?" DI Smyth asked.

"Dark blue," Derek replied.

"Are you absolutely sure about the name on the van?" DI Smyth said.

"Positive. You don't get a job as a firefighter without 20-20 vision. My eyes are as sharp now as they were twenty years ago."

"What time did the van leave?" DC Moore said.

"That I can't be a hundred percent sure about," Derek said. "But it was still there when I came up after my tea break at three, and it had gone by the time I'd finished working at five."

"What are you writing?" DI Smyth said.

"Nothing that anyone's going to want to read," Derek said and laughed. "It's a variation on the detective genre, only with a firefighter as the main character."

"It sounds intriguing."

"It helps to pass the time. I haven't got much else on."

"Are you not married?" DC Moore asked.

"Divorced," Derek said. "It's an occupational hazard in the fire service. Shift work and all that. You must see it in your line of work too."

"Is there anything else you can remember about the driver of the van?" DI Smyth said. "What about his height and build?"

"I wasn't paying much attention to him I'm afraid," Derek said. "But I don't think he was a big bloke. Not very tall and pretty thin."

"What about what he was carrying?" DC Moore said. "Could you see what it was he was delivering?"

Derek shook his head. "He was definitely carrying something, but I couldn't tell you what it was. I'm sorry I couldn't be more help."

"You've given us something to look into," DI Smyth said. "Thank you for your time."

"What happened?" Derek said. "There were police all over the place yesterday evening."

"A woman was killed," DI Smyth said.

He knew the truth would be out there soon, and he got the impression Derek James was someone who he could trust.

"Lockdown was good for something at least, wasn't it?" Derek sighed.

"We'll leave you in peace," DC Moore said.

"I'll see you out."

DI Smyth took out one of his cards and handed it to Derek. "If you do think of anything else, give me a call."

"I'll do that," Derek said. "And could you relay a message to that prat of a PC next time you see him? Tell him to consider going for an attitude transplant, because his attitude needs obliterating altogether."

"I'll pass on your comments," DI Smyth. "I'll pass them on with absolute pleasure."

CHAPTER NINE

Smith and DC King had spoken to three of the colleagues from Nunthorpe Primary School with whom Jennifer worked most closely, and all of them had told them the same thing. Jennifer was a well-regarded member of staff – the pupils and teachers alike all thought highly of her, and the news of her death had come as a great shock. None of them could think of any reason why someone would want to harm her. Smith had half-expected as much. He didn't think they were going to get the answers they needed from the teachers at a primary school.

"Does it feel good to be back, doing what you do best, Sarge?" DC King asked on the way back to the station.
"Asking the wrong questions to the wrong people?" Smith said.
"Investigating a murder. And you've said it yourself, you need to ask a lot of irrelevant questions before you can figure out the right ones to ask."
Smith studied her face. She wasn't aware of it because she was driving.
"Have you remembered every word I've ever spoken to you?"
DC King smiled. "Only the important ones. Sometimes you talk utter gibberish."
Smith smiled too. "It's only gibberish to people not wired the same way."
"That painting is important, isn't it?" DC King said.
She slowed down as the traffic light up ahead turned red.
"Definitely," Smith said. "Why leave it behind? The only reason to do that is because he wanted us to see it, but why? The woman was murdered – that's perfectly clear, so what does he stand to gain by leaving the portrait behind?"
DC King pulled away as the lights turned green. "What now?"
"I've run out of ideas," Smith said.

"It's still early days. Do you think this really is an isolated incident?"

"I sincerely hope it is," Smith said. "Generally when a sole victim is selected for a particular reason, we stand a better chance of catching the killer. Something always leads us back to them via the victim."

He took out his phone, swiped the screen and brought up the number for Dr Bean. The Head of Pathology answered straight away.

"Kenny," Smith said. "Sorry for bothering you."

"No you're not," Dr Bean said.

"Have you got anything for us?"

"You'll be the first to know when I have."

"How long are we talking about?" Smith asked.

"The postmortem is scheduled for two this afternoon. I'll have something for you before the end of the day."

"She was drugged. I'm positive she was drugged."

"If she was, we'll know. Will there be anything else? I was enjoying my lunch break."

"I'll let you get on," Smith said. "Thanks, Kenny."

He put the phone back inside his pocket and sighed deeply.

"Why do we always seem to be waiting for other people?"

"It can't be helped, Sarge," DC King said.

"Take the next left," Smith said.

They were approaching the Grimston Bar roundabout.

"That's the opposite direction to the station."

"I know," Smith said. "I just want to make a quick detour."

DC King indicated left and turned onto Hull Road.

"Where are we going?"

"I need to ask someone's opinion on the painting," Smith told her.

"An artist?"

"Not really, but she knows a thing or two about how the human brain works."

Smith hadn't seen Dr Fiona Vennell for a while. The young psychologist had been a major part of some of the past investigations, but the lack of crime recently meant they'd had no reason to speak. And Smith had been reluctant to get in touch after their last encounter when she'd expressed some veiled feelings for him. He knew it was probably better to keep his distance from her.

But now he needed her opinion on the painting the killer had left at the scene of the murder. It was possible she may be able to shed some light on why he'd left it in Jennifer Cole's lap. Smith knew instinctively there was a good reason for doing that.

"Do you want me to come in with you?" DC King asked.

Dr Vennell's practice was round the corner from the car park in Monk Bar.

"If you like," Smith said. "Do you have any cash for the meter?"

"I don't."

"Me neither," Smith said. "We'll risk it. We're on official police business anyway."

"Are we?"

"Sort of. Come on – I don't see any meter maids or whatever they call them these days."

They were in luck. The man behind the reception desk informed Smith that Dr Vennell didn't have any patients until three that afternoon. She was catching up with some paperwork in her office. Smith knocked on the door and he and DC King went inside.

Dr Vennell didn't even try to hide her pleasure at seeing Smith. The smile that appeared on her face was broad and genuine.

She stood up and walked up to him. "What brings you here?"
She leaned forward for a hug and Smith stepped back. He held out his hand instead and Dr Vennell shook it.

"I need you to take a look at something," he said. "You've met DC King, haven't you?"

Dr Vennell nodded and left it at that.

"What is it you want to show me?" she asked Smith.

"A photograph of a painting left at a crime scene," he said. "Is your email address still the same?"

"Of course."

Smith found the best photograph of the painting and frowned.

"How do I forward this to an email address?"

"Let me do it," DC King offered.

She tapped the screen a few times, confirmed Dr Vennell's email address and sent the photo.

"Considering you're in possession of the greatest detective brain this city has ever seen," Dr Vennell said. "You're rather inept in other areas."

"I've got two teenagers living with me," Smith said. "I don't need to worry about shit like that."

"Let's have a look, shall we?" Dr Vennell said and sat back down at her desk.

She opened the email and clicked on the attachment.

"I don't need to remind you this is confidential," Smith said.

Dr Vennell's raised eyebrow told him he didn't.

"What is it you need my opinion on?" she asked.

"This painting was left behind at the scene," Smith said. "I'm trying to figure out why."

"You're wondering why your killer didn't take it as a trophy?"

"I am. Why go to the trouble of painting it if you're just going to leave it behind?"

"I would have thought that was obvious."

"I did consider it was to send out a message," Smith said. "But what kind of message can be conveyed in a painting of a woman who was killed shortly after the painting was finished? It's basically an exact replication of the crime scene. I really don't understand the logic of leaving it behind."

Dr Vennell zoomed in on the painting.

"I'm particularly interested in why he bothered to add the painting above the fireplace in the portrait," Smith said.

"This is Barnard's *Maze of Chaos*."

"Who is Barnard?" DC King asked.

"Arno Barnard is a neo-modernist artist," Dr Vennell said. "The concept is rather confusing, and somewhat contradictory. Basically, neo-modernism strives to contrast to the complexity of post-modernist art, seeking greater simplicity. The *Maze of Chaos* was designed to be a parody of what neo-modernism is based on. Chaos is hardly simple, is it? The painting behind the dead woman is one of Barnard's."

"How come you know so much about this?" Smith asked.

"I did a couple of modules on modern art with my Psychology degree," Dr Vennell said.

"The painting with the roman numerals," Smith said. "The maze thing was on the wall in the room where the woman was killed. Why bother to include it in the portrait?"

"I really can't offer an opinion on that. But I can tell you without a shadow of a doubt that it was painted for a reason."

"Are you suggesting there's a message in that specific painting?" Smith said.

"Possibly. It's a rather captivating painting, isn't it?"

"I think so too," Smith agreed. "It draws you in."

DC King's phone started to ring. She took it from her pocket and looked at the screen.

"I have to take this," she said. "Excuse me."

"She has an unhealthy regard for you," Dr Vennell said when DC King had left the room.

"Kerry?" Smith said. "Rubbish."

"It's rather obvious. She worships the ground you walk on."

"I can't say I've noticed."

"Be careful," Dr Vennell warned. "Be very careful. Exaggerated hero-worship can be dangerous."

"For once, you're wrong, Dr Vennell," Smith said.

"OK. If you say so, and it's Fiona. You know that."

"Fiona," Smith humoured her. "Is there anything you can tell me about why the killer left that painting behind?"

"Not specifically, but there is a message in it somewhere. Who was the victim?"

"A primary school classroom assistant. Late-twenties. Girlfriend's an accountant. Perfectly normal women as far as I can see."

"Focus on that painting," Dr Vennell said.

"That's what I've been trying to tell the boss since we found it."

"It's good to see you again," Dr Vennell said. "I've missed you."

"It's been an unusual year," Smith said. "I'd better get going – we have a lot of work to do."

Dr Vennell got up and this time she was able to embrace him before he could stop her.

"Don't be a stranger, Jason. We must go for a drink sometime."

"I'd like that," Smith found himself saying.

His phone beeped in his pocket to tell him he'd received a message. He took it out and looked at the screen.

"Now I definitely have to go," he lied. "Work."
The message was actually a photograph of Andrew. The baby had pulled himself up using the chair in the kitchen and the photo showed him taking his first steps by himself.

CHAPTER TEN

Lionel Grange was in a foul mood. The restaurant he worked in as pastry chef had a function booked for tomorrow and the sous chef had forgotten to order the puff pastry for the apple strudel that was supposed to be served for dessert. The head chef didn't want to take a chance with supermarket bought pastry – he'd made that mistake before, so he told Lionel to go home to pick up the puff pastry he knew he had in his freezer there. He could be there and back within the hour. He'd have to wait for the puff pastry to defrost but he would still have enough time to prepare the strudel before the function.

Lionel owned a house a stone's throw away from the Minster in Garden Street. He'd inherited the place from his parents, and he now lived there with his fiancé Davina. She was the reason Lionel was in such a bad mood. He knew she would be at home, and he wasn't particularly keen to see her. They'd had a massive argument the previous night and Lionel had been happy to leave for work to get away from her for most of the day.

The house was only a five-minute walk from the restaurant, so Lionel lingered on the way. The head chef had given him an hour after all. He paused outside a travel agents and perused the offers in the window. He wasn't aware that there were any travel agencies left – most people he knew booked their holidays online, but the destinations on offer in the window showed that some people clearly like to organise their getaways the old-fashioned way.

A two-week deal to Thailand caught his eye. It was an all-inclusive package, and it was well within Lionel's budget. Davina had always talked about going to Thailand and the photographs of the beaches of Phuket in the window made Lionel feel guilty. The fight he'd had with his fiancé had been mostly his fault. He'd come off a long shift, he was dog-tired and he'd blown up about something insignificant. He wondered how long it would take to book the holiday.

Thirty minutes later Lionel stepped back outside into the sunshine. He patted the printout of the itinerary for the holiday in his pocket and smiled. If this wasn't an apology Davina would accept he didn't know what was. She was a teacher, and she wasn't due back at work for another five weeks. Two of those weeks would now be spent on the beaches of Thailand.

A quick glance at his watch told him he still had plenty of time to fetch the pastry and be back at the restaurant in time. He was almost home when his phone beeped in his pocket. He read the message and sighed. The sous chef had also neglected to order the tamarind for the prawn curry starter, and he was asking if Lionel had any at home. Lionel replied in the affirmative. He would bring that with the puff pastry.

He'd barely finished typing the message when a blue van screeched to a halt a couple of metres away from him. Lionel hadn't realised he'd crossed the road and typed the message at the same time. He raised his hands in apology and the van sped away. Lionel couldn't see the driver through the tinted windows.

The near miss with the van had shaken him so he took a moment to get his breath back. He was lucky the driver's reactions were quick. He walked up the path to his house, opened the door and went inside.

He smelled it immediately. It reminded him of when they'd painted the window frames in the house. The stench of the enamel paint had lingered for days. He wondered if Davina was doing a bit of DIY. She hadn't mentioned it to him.

He went straight to the kitchen. He would surprise his fiancé with the trip to Thailand after he'd fetched the puff pastry and tamarind. The smell of paint wasn't so strong in there. He put the pastry and spice in a bag and left it on the kitchen counter. He made his way to the living room and opened the door.

Two things became apparent when he went inside the room. The guests at tomorrow's function weren't going to get any apple strudel and Davina was never going to get the chance to visit Thailand.

* * *

"There's been another one."

Smith had lost count of how many times he'd heard those four words over the years. They were words that caused him mixed emotions. The human part of his brain would lament the loss of another human life, but the detective section of his brain would go through the motions to prepare him for what lay in store.

"What do we know?" he asked Baldwin.

Smith and DC King were halfway back to the station when he got the call. "A Lionel Grange called it in, in a bit of a state," Baldwin said. "He went home to find his fiancé dead in the living room. He didn't elaborate, but I dispatched some uniforms, and they confirmed it. They also mentioned something about a painting on the floor next to her body."

That was enough for Smith to tell him this murder was connected to the murder of Jennifer Cole.

He told DC King as much.

"Do you think this is the start of something?" she asked.

"I sincerely hope not," Smith said. "The address is number 16 Garden Street. You need to take the next right then it's the first left."

"What else do we know?" DC King said.

"As much as I've told you."

DC King parked outside number 16. A single police car was parked outside but that was it. For once Smith had beaten Grant Webber to the scene of a crime. Smith got out of the car and was immediately pounced on by PC Simon Miller.

"Sarge," he said. "It's not pretty in there."

Smith nodded. It never was.

"Has anyone else been inside?"

"Just myself and PC Griffin," PC Miller said.

"Great," Smith said. "That's all I need. Where is he?"

"Who, Sarge?"

"Griffin. Where is he?"

"With the fiancé. They're in the kitchen."

"Inside the house?"

Smith couldn't believe what he was hearing.

"That house is a crime scene," he said. "All of it. What the hell was PC Griffin thinking of?"

"The bloke refused to leave, Sarge," PC Miller said. "He made himself a cup of coffee and sat down in the kitchen. Then he started unpacking puff pastry. He kept babbling on about it needing to defrost. We tried to get him out, but he wouldn't budge. He started going on about how much Davina would have loved Thailand. He said he'd just booked a holiday to go there. PC Griffin offered to stay with him to make sure he didn't contaminate the scene any more than he already had."

Smith calmed down a bit. He reluctantly agreed that his latest nemesis had made the right call.

Webber didn't show up. Instead, Billie Jones and Pete Richards turned up in his place. Billie explained to Smith that her boss had a lot of work to get through back at the New Forensics Building but Smith doubted that was the real reason he didn't want to attend the scene of the murder. He knew it wasn't as simple as that. The wounds the Head of Forensics had suffered hadn't healed by a long shot, and Smith knew it would take a very long time before they did.

CHAPTER ELEVEN

"She was already dead when the painting was done."
DI Smyth had written Davina Hawkins' name on the whiteboard in the small conference room. Jennifer Cole's name was written next to it.
"It's the same killer though, isn't it?" DC King said.
"We don't know that."
"It's the same killer, boss," Smith insisted. "Almost identical MO. Both women were roughly the same age, they were alone in the house and a portrait of them was left at the scene. This is the same man beyond a shadow of a doubt."
"Unfortunately," DI Smyth said. "Miss Hawkins' fiancé wasn't able to tell us much. We managed to get him to leave the house, and he was taken to hospital. He's probably in shock but we'll be speaking to him as soon as he's up to it."

"What do we know about Davina?" Whitton asked.
"Forensics found some coursework from a school in Heworth," DI Smyth said. "She teaches Maths there."
"Another teacher," DC Moore said. "Do you think the connection is relevant?"
"No."
Smith didn't hesitate to come to that conclusion.
"It's worth looking into," DI Smyth said.
"These women weren't killed because of what they did for a living," Smith said.
"It needs to be considered," DI Smyth insisted.
"No, it doesn't," Smith said.

"What do we know about the fiancé?" Bridge asked.
"According to the man next door," DI Smyth said. "He's a chef at a restaurant not far from his house. We've spoken to the manager of the

restaurant and apparently the head chef asked him to go home to fetch some pastry."

"PC Miller said he was babbling on about having to defrost it," Smith remembered. "What time did he leave the restaurant?"

"About an hour before he called in about his dead fiancé," DI Smyth said.

"How far is the restaurant from his house?"

"It's a five-minute walk."

"Not enough time to kill her and paint the portrait then," DC Moore said.

"Unless he painted it beforehand," Smith said. "He lives with the woman, and it's possible that he planned this in advance. He needs to be questioned."

"It's highly unlikely that he killed her," DI Smyth said. "The woman suffered multiple stab wounds to her chest and neck. It would have been impossible to carry out an attack like that without getting some of her blood on himself. He was clean."

"The painting was slightly different this time," Smith said.

He'd asked Billie Jones to send him a photograph of it.

"She was definitely dead when she was painted on the canvas. The wounds and the blood are in the portrait."

DC Moore did his thing with the laptop and the painting appeared on the wide screen.

"Bloody hell," Bridge said. "This is some sick bastard."

Davina Hawkins had been stripped naked and positioned on a chair. Her eyes were open, but it was clear they weren't looking at anything. She had at least five lacerations to her chest and a couple more to her neck. The blood had dried and it was almost black.

"He waited quite some time before he painted her," Smith said. "And she definitely didn't get into that position without some help."

Her arms were resting on the side of the chair with the palms facing upwards. Her legs had been placed together, offering her some semblance of decency.

"Zoom in on her right leg," Smith said.

DC Moore obliged.

"What's that?" Bridge pointed to a brown smudge on her thigh.

"It's a fingerprint," Smith said. "He fucked up."

"It could have come from Davina herself," DC Moore pointed out.

"Whoever left it there," DI Smyth said. "Forensics will have seen it."

"The painting was left on the floor next to the chair," Smith said. "The portrait of Jennifer Cole was found in her lap."

"I don't think that's important," DI Smyth said. "What's important is he left it at the scene. Why did he do that?"

"There's hardly any background to this one," Smith noticed. "There's a crude depiction of the television behind her but nothing else. Hold on."

"What is it?" DI Smyth asked.

"Zoom in on that fingerprint again."

"What have you seen?" Whitton said.

"This isn't a crime scene photo," Smith said. "This is a painting of the crime scene."

"Why add the print?" DC King said.

"Exactly. Why do that?"

"If he painted it," DC King said. "It means he's noticed it."

"Which in itself implies he's not concerned about us tracking him down from it."

"He's not in the system," Whitton said. "And that's unusual. It's very rare for a killer who has demonstrated such brutality to have no previous record. They've usually been in trouble with the police in the past."

"The results from Jennifer Cole's postmortem will be in shortly," DI Smyth changed tack. "I'll see if I can fast-track the autopsy for Miss

Hawkins, and we'll know if she was drugged before she was killed. Harry and I got a lead of sorts from a man who lives in the same street as Jennifer Cole. Derek James is a retired firefighter, and he remembers seeing a dark blue courier van around the time of the murder."

"Couriers are not uncommon these days," Bridge said.

"This one was parked outside Jennifer's house for at least three hours."

"That is interesting," Smith said. "Did he see the driver?"

"He only got a brief glimpse of him. Nothing descriptive – short and slim, that was about it. He said he was carrying something, but he didn't see what it was."

"There was a logo on the side of the van," DC Moore said. "Harvey's Couriers."

"It'll be easy to find who it belongs to," Whitton said.

"I've never heard of them," Smith said.

"A load of new courier companies sprang up during the lockdowns," Bridge said. "We'll probably be able to find them on the Internet."

"Harvey's Couriers," DC Moore said.

He was looking at his mobile phone.

"They're a relatively new company running out of Heslington. For all your collection and delivery requirements – nothing too big and nothing too small. They've spelt the first *too* with one *o*."

"Smith," DI Smyth said. "Can you and Kerry go and speak to somebody there please?"

Smith didn't reply.

"Did you hear me?" DI Smyth said.

"I did, boss," Smith said. "But I don't think this bloke would travel to where he's planning on carrying out a murder in such an obvious vehicle."

"Perhaps that's the whole point," DC Moore said.

"You've lost me, Harry."

"DS Bridge is right," DC Moore said. "Courier vans are commonplace, and nobody pays them much attention. It's not unusual for a courier to be parked outside a house, so why would anyone think it was suspicious?"

"It needs checking out," DI Smyth said.

Smith nodded. "OK. That fingerprint is bothering me, boss. It's bothering me in the same way the Roman numeral painting bothered me in the first one. Both serve no purpose in the portraits. Why paint them?"

"I'm sure it will come to you in time," DI Smyth said.

"You're probably right. Come on, Kerry – let's head over to Heslington."

"When will your car be fixed?" Bridge said.

"Soon," Smith said.

"He's deluding himself." It was Whitton. "He won't admit that the time has finally come to put that car out of its misery."

CHAPTER TWELVE

The depot of Harvey's Couriers consisted of a small metal warehouse with a couple of prefabricated office buildings attached to it. A fleet of half a dozen blue vans were parked next to the warehouse. All of them had the same logo on the side – *Harvey's Couriers. For all your transport needs*. A mobile phone number was at the bottom of the sign. The windows of all the vans were tinted.

"It doesn't look like they're rushed off their feet," DC King commented. She parked in front of one of the prefabs.
"Perhaps this is a quiet time of year for courier companies," Smith said.
They got out of the car and walked up to the office building. Smith opened the door, and they went inside. A man was talking to someone on a mobile phone behind the desk. He gestured for them to take a seat and carried on with his call.

Smith took in the room. There wasn't much in it. A desk with a laptop on it stood against one of the walls. There were a couple of framed certificates on the wall behind the desk. Both of them were exactly the same apart from the dates. Harvey's Couriers had won the accolade of startup courier of the county for two years running. Smith wondered how much of an honour that actually was. There was a board on the wall with a number of car keys hanging on it.

The man ended his call and apologised for keeping them waiting. The badge on his shirt told them his name was John Harvey.
"What can I do for you?" he said. "Here at Harvey's we can help with all you transport needs."
Smith showed him his ID. DC King did the same.
"What's this all about?" John said. "Why are the police here?"
"Are you the owner of the company?" Smith asked him.

"Co-owner. My brother and I started the business a couple of years ago. And we're going from strength to strength."

"I couldn't help noticing the vans standing idle outside," Smith said. "How many vehicles do you run?"

"Eleven," John said. "We've got four on the road at the moment. Things have quietened down now that people are able to go out and get their own supplies. Things will pick up again once the novelty of being able to move around without restrictions has worn off."

"We want to talk to you about one of your vans," DC King said. "I assume you keep a record of your deliveries and pickups?"

"Of course," John tapped the top of the laptop. "Everything's on here, and I assure you everything is above board. We don't touch anything illegal."

"That's not why we're here," Smith said. "Yesterday, one of your vehicles was spotted in Murton. 45 Highfield Avenue. Would it be possible to check if you had a delivery to that address?"

"Don't you need a warrant?" John said.

"You're not obliged to give us what we're asking for," DC King said. "That's your right, but we would be grateful if you could check it for us. It would save us all a lot of time. Getting hold of a warrant for that kind of thing is time consuming, not to mention the headache of the full audit that will follow."

"Full audit?"

"In order to persuade the CPS to issue a warrant, we need to assure them we'll be conducting a thorough search. The last time we did that we wasted almost a week of time that could have been put to better use."

Smith was finding it hard not to laugh. He didn't think DC King had it in her, but her veiled threat seemed to have the desired effect.

"Highfield Avenue in Murton, you say?" John said.

He tapped the keypad on the laptop.

"That's correct," Smith said. "Between twelve and five yesterday afternoon."
"Nope," John said after a few seconds. "None of our vans were in Murton yesterday."
"Are you sure?" DC King said.
"Positive. There were no deliveries or collections there yesterday."
"We're going to need a list of all of your drivers," Smith said.
"What for?" John said.
"We're not obliged to tell you that. And this time we don't need a warrant. You *will* give us the names and contact details of everyone who has access to your vans. Obstruction of justice is a serious crime. Google it if you like."
"Do I need to call my lawyer?"
"Not unless you have something to hide," Smith said.
"This is outrageous. All of the employees at Harvey's Couriers undergo a strict security check. Some of the stuff we deliver is very valuable. I can assure you that none of my drivers are involved in anything dodgy."
"Could you print out that list please?" DC King said.
John tapped the keypad again and shortly afterwards a printer was brought to life at the back of the office.
"I can tell you now, none of my drivers are who you're looking for. We carry out background checks."
"So you said," Smith said.
"Harvey's Couriers do not employ people with criminal records."
Smith thought back to the smudged fingerprint on Davina Hawkins' thigh. The killer had painted it there even though it was unnecessary, and he concluded that the person they were looking for wasn't in their database.
"Where were you yesterday?" he asked.
"What?"
"Where were you between noon and five yesterday?" DC King said.

"Here," John told her. "I was here all day."

"Can anybody corroborate that?" Smith said.

"Some of the drivers will be able to. And the cameras outside will have caught me arriving and leaving."

He got up to get the printout of the list of employees. He handed it to Smith.

"Thank you."

Smith glanced at it and looked up at John.

"Your brother's name isn't on this list."

"He's not one of the drivers," John informed him.

"No," Smith said. "But he will have access to the vans. Where is he?"

"Off sick. Has been all week."

"We'll need his details," DC King said.

John sighed, grabbed the paper from Smith and wrote the address and phone number for Henry Harvey at the bottom of the list.

"Will there be anything else?" he said.

"I think that's all for now," Smith said. "Thank you for your cooperation."

"I didn't have much choice, did I?"

Smith and DC King walked back to the car. The six vans were still standing idle next to the warehouse.

"That must be costing them a bit," DC King said. "Having the majority of the fleet off the road."

Smith opened the car door and turned around.

"Where's the other van?"

"Sarge?"

"John Harvey told us they have eleven vans," Smith said. "Four are out on deliveries, and there are six here. Where's the other one?"

John didn't seem particularly pleased to see them again so soon.

"What now?"

"You said Harvey's Couriers has eleven vans," Smith said.

"That's right."

"There are six parked outside, and four out working – there's one unaccounted for."

"What?"

"One of your vans is missing," DC King said.

A quick check outside confirmed it. When John Harvey returned to the office, he looked furious.

"The bastards. Someone has nicked one of the vans."

"If it's the same one seen in Murton yesterday," Smith said. "It means it's been gone for over twenty-four-hours. Surely you would have noticed it by now."

"Clearly I didn't, did I? The bastards. The insurance is going to rocket after this. Do I need to file some kind of report?"

"That doesn't concern us," Smith said. "What does concern us is the fact that one of your vans was seen close to where a serious crime was committed. You mentioned something about CCTV."

"Of course," John's face lit up. "The cameras will have caught the bastards in the act."

The smile was wiped off his face soon afterwards, and Smith was equally disappointed. The CCTV cameras did catch the moment where the van was stolen from the yard, but the quality was grainy and all they could make out was a dark figure creeping up to the van on the far right. It took them less than a minute to get inside, start the engine and drive away from the warehouse.

CHAPTER THIRTEEN

The van was found later that afternoon. It had been abandoned on a piece of open ground not far from the A64. There was no damage to the vehicle and the mystery as to how that was possible was cleared up quickly. All of the keys to the vans were kept on a board in the office, and one of the sets was missing. John Harvey hadn't noticed that either.

It was quite clear that the footage from the CCTV cameras wasn't going to give them much of an idea what the person who stole the van looked like. The footage had been analysed and the best shot of the van thief the tech team could get by enhancing the image wasn't anything that would help them. All it showed was a hooded figure of average height. There were no facial features and not even an idea about the sex of the thief. All hope now lay with the Forensics team. The van was in their hands and everyone on the team were praying that the perpetrator had left something behind.

"Are we working on the assumption that the perp is a man?" DC Moore asked.

DI Smyth had called a briefing, and the team were gathered once more in the small conference room.

"I think it's safe to make that assumption, Harry," DI Smyth said. "And we'll refrain from using that term. Perp is so American. Does anyone disagree?"

"About what?" Smith said. "About the use of American cliches, or about jumping to conclusions far too soon."

"Are you suggesting that a woman could be responsible for what was done to Jennifer Cole and Davina Hawkins?" Bridge asked him.

"I'm just reminding you of how dangerous it is to assume the most obvious scenario. It is possible we're looking for a woman."

"Do you think we are?" DI Smyth said.

"No," Smith said. "I don't think a woman did this."
"There's something seriously wrong with your brain, mate," Bridge said.
"Thank you. The violence on display at the crime scenes strikes me as something a man would be responsible for, but we live in strange times and anything's possible. We need to keep an open mind."

"We've got the results of the postmortem," DI Smyth said. "Jennifer Cole was definitely drugged before she was killed. Dr Bean found traces of a strong benzodiazepine in her blood. More of the same sedative was discovered in the residue in the wine glass and in the bottle itself. Miss Cole will probably have been oblivious to what happened to her afterwards."
"That's something at least," Whitton said.
"What else did Kenny find?" Smith asked.
"Time of death was between one and four yesterday afternoon," DI Smyth said.
"Couldn't he be more precise?" DC Moore said.
"What for?" Smith said. "I'd say a three-hour window is enough."
"And it ties in with the time the van was parked outside the house," Whitton said. "The killer is definitely the same person who stole that van."
"Webber will make the van a priority," DI Smyth said.

"Are we still going to look into the drivers of Harvey's Couriers?" DC Moore wondered.
"We are," DI Smyth confirmed. "There was no report of a break in at the office in Heslington so it's possible it was an inside job. I find it hard to believe the killer would know about the keys inside the office. I'll put some uniforms on it. The employees may not be directly involved, but it's possible someone may have spoken about where the keys to the vans are usually kept."

"We need to speak to the husband of the second victim," Smith said.
"Fiancé," DC Moore corrected.

"We need to speak to him."

"He's still in hospital," Bridge said.

Smith frowned at him. "I know where the hospital is. I'll speak to him there."

"He's not involved," DI Smyth said. "The carnage inside 16 Garden Street will have taken some time to pull off. The time between Mr Grange leaving the restaurant and reporting the murder wasn't enough to be able to carry out something like this."

"I'm running out of ideas, boss," Smith said.

"It's still early days."

"And two women are dead."

"We're doing everything we can. We have the vehicle that was almost definitely used by the killer, and it's highly unlikely he will have left nothing behind in there. Webber will find something. It's getting late, so I suggest you all go home and get some rest. We're all exhausted."

As if to emphasise this Bridge stretched his arms and yawned. Smith got to his feet and left the room. He went outside and took out his cigarettes. He lit one and looked up at the sky. The sun was going down over the Minster to the west. Soon it would fall behind the old spires. Smith thought it would make a great subject for a painting when the golden orb was directly behind the ancient cathedral. The lighting would be perfect. He took a long drag on his cigarette and reached inside his pocket for his phone. He brought up the photos he'd taken inside Jennifer Cole's house. Then he looked at the one Billie Jones had taken of the scene of Davina Hawkins' murder. Smith didn't know much about art but even he could see that the paintings looked like they'd been painted by two different artists. The one depicting the backdrop of the chaos maze was intricate and it looked like someone had taken great care in creating it, but the painting of Davina Hawkins seemed almost amateurish in comparison. The artist was talented – there was no doubt about that, but this painting didn't show the same flair as the one of Jennifer. Smith wasn't sure what this meant. He knew it was virtually impossible to consider they were dealing with two killers with this particular MO, but what if that's exactly what this was? It didn't bear thinking about.

The screen on his phone told him it was just before seven. It was almost visiting time at the hospital. Smith stubbed out his cigarette and went to find Whitton. He needed a lift.

CHAPTER FOURTEEN

Lionel Grange was sitting up on the bed in the ward Smith and Whitton had been directed to. The sister they'd spoken to told them he'd been given the green light to go, and he was just waiting for a doctor to come and sign the discharge paperwork. Whitton had argued on the way there that they were wasting their time. DI Smyth was right, and there was no possible way that Lionel could get from the restaurant and carry out such a brutal attack in the time he was gone. Smith had retorted with a typical comeback.
It's always the husband, isn't it?

"Are you a doctor?" Lionel asked him when he approached the bed.
"Do I look like a doctor?" Smith said.
"Not really."
"My name is Jason Smith. And this is Erica Whitton. We're detectives with York CID. Can we have a quick word?"
"Can you make it quick?" Lionel said. "My sister is coming to pick me up."
"It'll be as quick as it needs to be," Smith informed him. "We could reschedule if you prefer. At a time more convenient for you."
"That would be great."
"Of course, you'll have to come in and be formally interviewed at the station. I assume you have a lawyer."
"OK," Lionel said. "What do you want to know?"
"You work as a chef in a restaurant, don't you?" Smith said.
"A pastry chef," Lionel said. "There's a big difference."
"And today," Whitton said. "You'd run out of pastry, so you went home to get some."
"I didn't run out – the sous chef forgot to put it on the order."
"Is it common for you to fetch ingredients from home?" Smith asked.

"It happens from time to time. I only buy the best for my personal use, and the head chef knows this. He refuses to use supermarket bought ingredients."

"What time did you leave the restaurant?" Smith said.

"Just after eleven."

"And you went straight home?"

"Yes," Lionel said. "I mean no. I saw an ad in the window of a travel agency for a deal on a holiday to Thailand and I booked it on a whim. Davina has always wanted to go there. We'd had a fight, and I thought it would be the ideal apology. Only now she'll never know I was sorry will she? I can't believe it happened. I really don't…"

He stopped there. Smith was worried he was going to cry, but he didn't.

"Do you have any proof of this holiday booking?" he asked.

Lionel reached inside the jacket on the back of the chair and took out the sheet of paper with the itinerary on it. He handed it to Smith.

Smith read it and nodded. "This was printed at 11:42."

"That's right. I was surprised by how quickly a holiday can be booked. Why are you asking me about the holiday to Thailand?"

"Detective Sergeant Smith likes to ask a lot of questions about a lot of things," Whitton said.

"When you arrived home," Smith said. "Did you notice anything suspicious?"

"What do you mean?" Lionel said.

"Anyone acting strangely. Someone you hadn't seen before."

"Not really. Although I almost got knocked over."

"A car nearly drove into you?" Whitton said.

"A van. It was my fault. The sous chef sent me a message asking if I could bring some tamarind back with me too, and I didn't realise I was crossing the road when I typed a reply back. We're obsessed with our phones these days, aren't we?"

"What did this van look like?" Smith said.

"I didn't pay it much attention."

"Had you seen it before?" Whitton said.

"Not that I recall. It was just a van. I gestured to the driver that I was sorry, but I couldn't tell if he'd seen me through the tinted windows."

Smith looked at Whitton and she nodded.

"Can you describe this van?" he asked Lionel.

"It was an ordinary dark blue van. There was something written on the side, but I didn't see what it was. Why are you asking me about the van?"

Smith didn't tell him.

"Do you know if anyone on your street has CCTV cameras?" he asked instead.

"There are a few cameras further up the road," Lionel said.

"Is it possible the van was a courier van?" Smith said.

"I suppose so. Why are you so interested in the van? It nearly knocked me over. That's all."

A woman came inside the room. She introduced herself as Dr Wilson and Smith asked her if she could give them another five minutes.

"How are you feeling?" he asked Lionel.

"What?"

"How are you feeling?"

"How do you think I'm feeling?" Lionel said. "I just came home to find my fiancé... Slaughtered. That's the only way to describe it. How the fuck do you think I'm feeling?"

"I think we can finish there," Whitton suggested.

Smith nodded in agreement.

"Will you be staying with your sister tonight?" he asked Lionel.

"Your lot didn't give me much choice," Lionel said.

"Unfortunately," Whitton said. "The house is still a crime scene, and therefore it's off-limits. The team will try to be as quick as possible."
"We're going to need your sister's details," Smith said.
Lionel glared at him. "What the hell for?"
"Just in case we need to get hold of you again."
"I gave my phone number to the PC earlier."
"I'm sure that'll be sufficient," Whitton said. "We'll be in touch."
"We will," Smith added.

"What was that all about?" Whitton asked as they were driving home.
"What was what about?" Smith said.
"You were a bit hard on him."
"He didn't do it."
"I know he didn't do it," Whitton said. "You could have used a bit more tact. The man has just lost his fiancé."
"I just needed to make absolutely sure he wasn't involved. He was a bit too calm under the circumstances, and that made me a bit suspicious. I'm satisfied now – he had nothing to do with Davina's murder."
"I'm starting to worry about you," Whitton said.
"Don't be. What do feel like eating tonight?"

CHAPTER FIFTEEN

It was put to the vote and the unanimous decision in the Smith household was for pizza. Whitton was in the shower when the pizza was delivered, and Smith wasn't sure how he would be able to pay for the food. The young woman looked at him as though he'd grown another head when he explained his problem.
"It was ordered using the app," she reminded him.
"Was it?"
This was news to Smith. Lucy had put in the order, and he assumed she'd phoned and told them what they wanted.
"I still need to pay for it," he said.
"Your credit card details are on the app. It was paid for when it was ordered."
This was also news to Smith. He wasn't even sure his credit card was still up to date. It had been so long since he'd used it.

The groans coming from the kitchen told him the discussion with the delivery woman was taking too long. There were four hungry kids waiting for their pizza. Fran Rogers from next door was having a sleepover with Laura. Smith thanked the delivery woman and took the pizza through to the kitchen to feed the masses.

Twenty minutes later all that was left on the table was a solitary slice of pepperoni pizza. Darren Lewis and Laura were engaged in a Mexican standoff on opposite sides of the table. Finally, Darren reached for the slice, made a play of taking a bite and handed it to Laura. The smile she thanked him with made Smith grin like an idiot.

"Would you be able to look after Andrew tonight?" Lucy asked.
"The new *Purge* film is showing at the cinema," Darren elaborated.
"We'll look after him," Laura offered.

"What's this *Purge* film about?" Smith asked.

"It's part of a series," Lucy said. "Once a year, from seven at night until seven in the morning all crime is legalised."

"What?" Smith said. "And people go to watch shit like that?"

"It's a really interesting premise," Lucy said. "The concept is genius, and it really makes you think."

"What would you do if all crime was legal, Mr Smith?" Darren said.

"All crime you say?" Smith said.

"Everything. Robbery, grand theft auto, and even murder. Who would you kill if you knew you could get away with it?"

"I think this conversation has run its course," Whitton decided.

"No," Smith said. "Darren has raised an interesting point. Who would I kill? I'll have to think about that."

"Jason," Whitton warned.

"What's a premise?" Laura asked.

Everybody laughed. The sound of Andrew's wails upstairs told them the baby needed attention. Laura and Fran were out of the room in a flash.

Lucy and Darren went after them. Smith took two beers out of the fridge, opened them both and handed one to Whitton. He sat back down and took a long swig from the bottle.

"There are only a few beers left," he said. "I forgot to buy more."

"I'm sure you'll survive," Whitton said.

"Have you seen the *For Sale* sign next door?" Smith said.

"I noticed it when we came home," Whitton said. "I wonder what's going to happen to Sheila and Fran."

"Do you think she might consider buying the place?"

"I'm not sure if she can afford it. That's why she was renting."

"I doubt it'll sell quickly anyway," Smith said. "It's not like this is one of the more desirable areas of the city."

"You'd be surprised," Whitton said. "*For Sale* signs don't stay up long around here."

"Those paintings are really bugging me," Smith said. "Why go to all that effort only to leave them behind?"

"Put it out of your mind."

"I need to know why he left them there," Smith said. "Dr Vennell reckons it's important."

Whitton raised an eyebrow. "When did you speak to her?"

"Kerry and me went to see her. I needed her opinion on the paintings."

"What else did she say?"

"Not much," Smith said. "But she told me to focus on those paintings."

"We can worry about that tomorrow."

"No," Smith said and stood up. "I can do it right now. I want to know why he painted them."

He left the room and returned with his laptop. He switched it on and got another beer out of the fridge.

"I'm going out for a smoke while it boots up. That thing takes forever."

The air was warm when Smith stepped outside to the back garden. He could smell something cooking – one of the neighbours was having a barbecue, and the smoke was drifting across the gardens. The odour triggered a memory from Smith's childhood. It was summer and he was in his early teens. His sister Laura was helping their father cook some sausages on the grill outside. Someone was playing the guitar in the garden next door and the atmosphere was upbeat.

That was before everything went wrong. It was before Smith's dad chose to hang himself from a tree in the garden. Smith would be the one to find him, swinging in the breeze on Christmas Day. His sister would go next – she would be taken from a beach and Smith would blame himself for years afterwards. Barbecues were never the same after that.

Lucy came outside with Andrew. The spark in the baby's eyes when he spotted his granddad burst the bubble of melancholy inside Smith's head in an instant, and when the one-year-old held out his arms the seasoned detective melted. He reached out for his grandson and took him from Lucy.

"Shit," he said to her. "What have you been feeding him?"

"Nothing but good stuff," she said.

"Well he weighs a ton."

"Would you mind watching your language around Andrew?"

"No worries," Smith said, and whispered to his grandson. "Your mother doesn't want your first word to be, *shit*."

"I heard that."

Lucy's tone was serious, but she was smiling.

The laptop had warmed up when Smith sat behind it. He'd left Andrew in the capable hands of Laura and Fran Rogers. Whitton had told him she wanted to relax in front of the television. Smith didn't know where to start looking. He opened his email and saved the attachments the photos had been sent in. He had a photograph enhancing program that he was fairly comfortable with so he opened that up and pasted the first photograph into the *new project* option on the screen.

He wasn't quite sure what he was looking for. Jennifer Cole was looking directly at the artist. Smith zoomed in and cropped the shot so the background filled the screen. The painter had captured the neo-modernist artwork in great detail and Smith still couldn't understand why he had bothered to do this. The Roman numerals seemed to have been painted randomly, and Smith wondered if that was the intention of the artist who'd painted the original piece.

He tried to recall the name of the artist but no matter how hard he tried to remember, the name eluded him. He picked up his phone and sent Fiona Vennell as short message asking her about it. Shortly afterwards his phone beeped. The laptop followed suit. A notification at the top of the screen told Smith he'd received a new email. He would read that later.

"Arno Barnard," Smith read the name Dr Vennell had sent him. "*The Maze of Chaos.*"

He ignored the two kisses at the end of the message. He minimised the screen and opened up his browser. After keying the artist and the work into the taskbar, an image of the painting appeared on the screen. Smith copied it, opened the photograph enhancer and pasted it next to the photo of the portrait of the crime scene.

His initial impression was that the recreation of Barnard's work was identical but when he looked more closely, he realised there were some subtle differences. They were barely noticeable but they were there. Some of the Roman numerals were different, and others had been placed upside down. Smith didn't think this was important. The piece was an intricate one, and it would be almost impossible to replicate it exactly.

But then something occurred to him. He zoomed in on the painting the killer had created.

"He used her blood to finish off the painting."

The Roman numerals that were at odds with the ones in the original piece had been added using Jennifer Cole's blood.

Smith didn't have any theories about why this was, nor was he any the wiser as to whether the numerals were random or not. It was impossible to tell. Some of them were upside down and others had been painted sideways. It didn't make any sense. Smith finished his beer and took another one out of the fridge.

He decided not to waste any more time on the photograph of Jennifer Cole and instead he turned his attention to the photo of the painting of the Davina Hawkins murder. The flashing email icon caught his attention as he was closing the photo of Jennifer, so he opened it up to see who it was from.

He raised the bottle of beer to his lips, but he was stopped mid-drink when he read the words on the screen.

Detective Smith.

We've never met, but you know who I am.

I'm offering you my help.

You can stop me – everything you need is right in front of your face, but you have to know where to look.

Smith managed to take a sip of the beer. He read the email again and composed a short reply.

Who is this?

The reply arrived less than a minute later, and it consisted of just six words.

You can call me The Painter.

CHAPTER SIXTEEN

"*The Painter*," Bridge said.

Smith had brought up the email first thing in the morning briefing. He'd been unable to sleep, and his thoughts had consisted of nothing else as he tossed and turned. He still didn't know what to make of the bizarre email.

"It sounds like a nut job," DC Moore said. "Someone who's read about the details of the murders."

"As far as I'm aware," DI Smyth said. "The details of the crime scenes aren't common knowledge. The identities of the victims are out there, but the paintings aren't."

"You know what it's like, sir," Bridge said. "News spreads quickly these days. For all we know someone could have leaked the bit about the paintings."

"Who?" Smith said. "The only people who were privy to that information are the people on this team."

"It could have been the partners of the victims," DC King suggested. "Stranger things have happened."

"We need to find out," DI Smyth said.

"No," Smith disagreed. "The wording in the email doesn't strike me as something an attention seeker would write."

"Is there any way we can trace the email?" Whitton wondered. "I thought all addresses were linked to a service provider."

"There are many ways to mask an email address these days," DC Moore told her. "You can create an encrypted address with an anonymity-focused provider in a matter of seconds."

"What about the tech team?" Smith said. "Surely they can get past that."

"I doubt it," DC Moore said. "It's virtually impossible, and the scary thing is, the man in the street now has access to this kind of technology."

"What did this Painter mean?" DC King said. "Everything you need is right in front of your face. What does that even mean?"

"I have no idea, Kerry," Smith admitted.

"Have you had any further correspondence from this person?" DI Smyth asked.

"Nothing," Smith said. "How did they even get my email address?"

"What address was it?" DC Moore said. "Work or home?"

"It was my personal email. What difference does it make?"

"We might be able to narrow it down a bit. How many people have that address?"

"God knows," Smith said.

"We'll put the email on the backburner for now," DI Smyth decided.

"I think *The Painter* is our killer, boss," Smith said.

"And we will revisit that line of enquiry, but for now we need to focus our attention elsewhere. The list of the employees of Harvey's Couriers didn't yield much. All but one of them can account for their whereabouts for the time of at least one of the murders. Half of them were working, and the GPS in the vans can confirm where they were, and the others all have solid alibis."

"Who is the one who can't account for his whereabouts?" Smith asked.

"Henry Harvey. He's the co-owner of the courier company."

"According to his brother he's been off sick all week," Smith remembered. "John Harvey told us he hasn't been at work. He's our first port of call."

"I agree," DI Smyth said. "He has access to those vans. He will have a key to the portacabin where the keys to the vans are kept, and he knows where the CCTV cameras are located."

"We've got his details," Smith said. "I'll go and pay him a visit after the briefing."

"Forensics are still busy with the van that was abandoned," DI Smyth said. "But we do have something more from a pathology perspective. Dr Bean confirmed that Davina Hawkins had a large quantity of the same sedative found in Jennifer Cole in her system. Both women were drugged before they were killed."

"Anything else?" Smith asked.

"Davina's time of death was sometime between nine and noon yesterday, and, unlike Jennifer, there were indications that she put up a fight. Dr Bean found what looked like defensive wounds on both hands."

"She was taken by surprise," Smith said. "I think she opened the door to someone posing as a courier, he attacked her, and she tried to defend herself."

"The blood found in the hallway would suggest this," DI Smyth said. "And I'm confident Forensics will find traces of blood in the van."

"They will," Smith agreed. "The van was used in both murders."

"We don't know that yet," DC Moore said.

"I do," Smith insisted.

"We spoke to Davina's fiancé at the hospital last night," Whitton told them.

"He's not involved," Smith said. "He booked a holiday to Thailand, and he only left the travel agency at around 11:45. He showed us the itinerary he was given. But he did mention something interesting. He was distracted by his phone when he was crossing the road, and he told us a van almost ran him over. It was a dark blue van with tinted windows."

"It has to be the same van," Bridge said.

"It's definitely the same one. It was in the area at the time of the murder."

"What are the odds on that?" DC King said. "The fiancé of the woman who was murdered almost getting knocked over by her killer?"

"We need uniforms back in Garden Street," Smith said. "Lionel Grange mentioned CCTV cameras in the street. We might get lucky and find someone who has security cameras that actually serve a purpose. What is the point in having CCTV if the image quality is so poor you can't make out anything about the people caught on camera?"

"I think we've covered everything for now," DI Smyth said.

"Me and Kerry will head over to the courier company co-owner," Smith told him.

DI Smyth nodded. "Bridge, I want you, Whitton and Harry to focus on the paintings."

"What are we supposed to be looking for?" DC Moore asked.

"I'm no expert on art, but even I can see that both paintings were done by a very talented artist."

"It's possible he's exhibited his work somewhere in the past," Bridge said.

"That's right," DI Smyth said. "Speak to people at the galleries in the city. Someone might recognise something in the style he uses."

"I assume we're taking the paintings seriously then," Smith said.

"As far as I'm aware, I've never completely disregarded them."

"You're the boss."

"Don't forget it," DI Smyth said. "And as the boss, I now have the pleasure of a meeting with Chalmers and the Super to discuss our progress."

"It's been two days," Bridge said. "What do they expect us to have figured out in two days?"

"Tell Uncle Jeremy we're close to a breakthrough," Smith advised.

"We're nowhere near that stage," DI Smyth said.

"It'll shut him up for a while."

"I'll bear that in mind," DI Smyth said. "And how many times do I have to remind you it's Superintendent Smyth to you."

"I'll try to remember that in future," Smith said.

CHAPTER SEVENTEEN

Grant Webber wasn't in a great place. He glanced at the canvas on the table and got to his feet. He couldn't bear to look at it any longer. He removed his gloves and walked over to the counter where the kettle and microwave stood. He needed a strong cup of coffee. He boiled the kettle and put three spoons of coffee into his mug. He added two spoons of sugar and rubbed his eyes. He hadn't slept well since he'd witnessed what had been done to Jennifer Cole and it was starting to take its toll.

He needed some fresh air, so he took the coffee outside. Billie Jones came out shortly afterwards.
"Are you OK?"
Webber held up the coffee. "I will be after drinking this."
"Do you want to talk about it?"
"No," Webber said.
Billie knew better than to press him further, but she did anyway.

"You don't have to take the brunt of the work on this one," she said. "I'm more than happy to do a bit more if you want to take a step back."
"I appreciate your concern, Billie," Webber said. "But I am more than capable of separating my emotions from my work."
"I don't doubt that, but you're still human, and you don't have to put yourself through this. Everyone will understand if you need to take some time off."
"What are you implying?" Webber's tone had turned aggressive.
"I have the utmost respect for you," Billie said. "You're one of the finest forensics experts in the country, but I heard about what happened and I don't think it's healthy for you to take on too much in this investigation."
Webber turned to face her. "I really do appreciate your concern, Billie, but I'm fine."

"OK," she said. "I'm not finished with the courier van, but I did find what appears to be blood on the driver's seat and the dashboard. We'll know if it came from either of the victims before the end of the day."

"Anything else?"

"No painting materials, but I did detect an odour inside. I think it's paint. Oil based paint. And there is a smudge on the steering wheel that was still sticky to the touch. I think it's paint."

"So, we're onto something with the van?"

"Without a shadow of a doubt," Billie confirmed. "Pete is still busy analysing the print found on Davina Hawkins' thigh. Smith is convinced it won't be on file."

"Smith may be a lot of things," Webber said. "But he's rarely wrong. I'm inclined to agree with him. The killer added the print to the painting, and he would not do that if he knew we'd be able to find him via his fingerprint. We're not going to get anything from that print."

"Are you sure you're OK?"

"Yes."

She remained where she was.

"Really," Webber added. "I'm fine, and I wouldn't mind five minutes alone if that's alright with you."

He watched her go back inside and sat down on the wall outside the entrance to the building. He sipped the coffee and closed his eyes. He wasn't fine. He was far from fine, and he knew that Billie Jones was correct in voicing her concerns. This investigation was still in its infancy, but it had already affected him deeply. The demons he'd managed to keep buried had reared their ugly heads once more, and he knew he ran the risk of being consumed by them.

But he didn't have it in him to admit that he wasn't up to the job. He'd been a forensic investigator for half his life now, and it was all he knew.

Something occurred to him, and he didn't know how to interpret it. Yesterday, when the call had come in about the murder in Garden Street he hadn't hesitated to remain behind while Billie and Pete Richards attended the scene. What occurred to him now was the fact that this was probably the first time he'd ever done that, and he wasn't sure what to think about it.

He wasn't given a chance to dwell on it. Pete Richards came outside to find him.

"I think you ought to take a look at something," he said.

"What is it?" Webber asked.

"I need a second opinion about the print we got from Davina Hawkins' leg."

Webber nodded. He finished his coffee and followed his technician back inside.

"What have you found?" Webber asked Billie Jones.

She was looking at the screen of the laptop.

"I showed her what I'd found when I realised there was something wrong," Pete said.

On the screen was a close up of the photograph of the fingerprint found on Davina Hawkins' right thigh.

"It's not a fingerprint," Billie said.

Webber took a closer look. "It looks like a print to me."

"I think it's a transfer," Pete told him.

"Transfer?"

"Like those tattoo things you used to get in chewing gum packets," Billie said. "The ones you peel off and apply to the skin. They were popular with kids."

"It looks like a print to me," Webber said.

"I think it's supposed to," Billie said. "And I agree it does have the ridges and troughs of an ordinary fingerprint, but there's something else there too."

"If you look at it from another angle," Pete said. "You can see something else in there."

He tapped the keypad, and the image was turned upside down.

"Good Lord," Webber said. "Zoom in."

Pete obliged and what they believed to be a fingerprint now looked like something entirely different.

"It looks like a face," Webber said.

"I think so too," Billie said. "It's a transfer of a face."

The features of the face weren't very clear but there was a definite symmetry to the image. The eyes were large, and the nose small, and the thin lips of the person on the screen were pressed together as if they'd been glued into place. The face was framed by thick black curls.

"What do you think it means?" Billie asked Webber.

"It beats me," he said. "Perhaps this was transferred to the victim before the murder. We have no way of knowing if it's even connected to the death of Davina Hawkins."

"It looks like a cartoon character," Pete said. "One of those old-fashioned ones."

"I think so too," Billie said. "How could it be connected? You're right – it was probably there long before she was killed."

CHAPTER EIGHTEEN

Paula Burton had never been happy with the way she looked. Ever since she was a little girl she'd been teased about her appearance. Her large brown eyes looked too big for her face and the tiny nose only served to enhance their size. Her lips were thin, and she'd always longed for straight hair. She detested the thick black curls that she could never seem to straighten.

The teasing had started from an early age. When she was in junior school, she was called all the names under the sun, but the one that stuck was *Betty Boop* after the old cartoon character. Paula's mother had tried to make things better by telling her that *Betty Boop* was actually a depiction of a pretty woman and she ought to take what the other children were telling her as a compliment, but Paula didn't see it that way. And when the insults became more personal in secondary school, she was determined to do something about her appearance one day when she was able to afford it. Paula developed unfortunately large breasts at an early age, and the innocent nickname morphed into something more hurtful. She couldn't wait to leave school and put her *Betty Boobs* days behind her.

Paula studied her reflection in the mirror in the hallway. "One day," she looked into her large brown eyes.
She would start with her lips. There were all sorts of ways to make them fuller and it wasn't as expensive as it once was. Her breasts would be more of a problem, but she'd heard that certain breast reduction surgeries were covered by the NHS if she was able to demonstrate that a certain degree of physical debilitation resulted from their abnormal size. Paula was a short woman, and she'd started to suffer from back problems. All she needed was proof that those problems were due to the weight of her chest putting pressure on her spine, and she was sure she would be approved for the surgery.

She took a final look at herself in the mirror and put on her coat. She swiped the screen of her phone and checked the address again. She was due there in thirty minutes. The flyer had caught her attention straight away when she'd found it in her postbox. Paula had always wanted to have her portrait painted, and this one wouldn't cost her anything if she played her cards right. The person she'd replied to had told her there would be no charge if she wasn't happy with the painting.

She had some reservations about meeting a complete stranger at his house, but she didn't get the impression that the person who replied to her messages was a threat to her. She'd been given the choice of location – the artist was happy to paint her anywhere she chose, and the clincher was when she was informed that she was welcome to bring somebody with her if she was worried.

She'd debated it, but the feeling she'd got from the messages was a positive one. And she really didn't want any of her friends to be there when she was having her portrait painted. It was something intimate and it was something she wanted to enjoy alone. She would get her painting, and it would cost her nothing. She would tell the artist that this one was a *before* portrait. After she'd changed her appearance, she would return for the second one. She would pay for both paintings when she came back to get the *after* one done. Of course she had no intention of doing any such thing, but he didn't need to know that.

The address she'd been given was a house close to Hull Road. The majority of properties in that area were used to house students from the nearby university and Paula knew it well from her time there. She'd completed two years of a history degree but failed to finish because of money problems. She planned to return one day when her financial situation improved.

She passed the pizza shop and spotted someone she knew walking towards her on the opposite side of the road. It was a woman she recalled from university, and she wondered what she was still doing in the city. Paula couldn't remember her name. She'd seen her too, and she was crossing the road.

"Paula," she said. "Long time."

"It's been a while. Good to see you again."

"You don't remember me, do you?"

"Of course I do," Paula said. "You were in my history class. I'm afraid I've forgotten your name though. My memory never was that great."

"Is that why you ditched the history degree? It's Kate."

"Of course," Paula said. "I'd better be going. I have an appointment."

"Nothing serious I hope?"

"It's not that kind of appointment. I'm getting my portrait painted."

Kate raised an eyebrow at this.

"It's for a friend's portfolio," Paula lied. "She needs to build it up before her final year of art college."

"Oh, right. I'll let you get on. It was good to see you again."

Paula walked away before she started up the conversation again. She crossed over the road by the Milson Grove bus stop and turned right onto Norman Street. The painter had told her to ring the bell of number 13. The street was quiet. It was the summer holidays and many of the university students had gone home. Paula wondered if the painter was an art student, and she suddenly felt guilty about her intentions. Perhaps she ought to pay for the portrait after all. She remembered all too well how difficult it had been to make ends meet during her student days.

Number 13 Norman Street was a typical mid-terrace property. Paula knew from experience that it would consist of two bedrooms, a lounge, bathroom and kitchen. She'd set foot in many similar houses in her time.

She stopped outside the door and pressed the bell. A dog started to bark somewhere close by and Paula turned around. She watched the small brown dog as it ran past the house and raced up the street. Shortly afterwards a middle-aged man ran by. He was holding a dog lead in his hand. He cast a glance in Paula's direction and carried on chasing his dog up the road. Later, when questioned by York CID he would express regret for not stopping the young woman from going inside the house.

CHAPTER NINETEEN

The first thing that occurred to Smith when the man opened the door for himself and DC King was he didn't look particularly ill. The second thing that crossed his mind was the young man looked absolutely nothing like John Harvey. He wondered if he'd been given the correct address.

"Henry Harvey?" he said.

"That's me. You must be from the police. Our John said you'd be popping round. Come in."

Smith looked at DC King and they followed Henry inside. He told them to take a seat in the living room and went to make some coffee without offering first.

"He doesn't seem too bothered by us being here," DC King whispered to Smith.

"Don't let that fool you," Smith said.

DC King sat down but Smith remained standing. It was a fair-sized room but there wasn't much in it. A two-seater sofa and a leather armchair were the only seats, and apart from a coffee table and a gigantic flatscreen TV screen there wasn't much else inside the room. There were no pieces of furniture with ornaments on them and nothing whatsoever on the walls. Smith deduced that Henry Harvy was single and he lived alone.

Henry came in and placed a tray of coffee onto the table.

"Help yourself."

Neither Smith nor DC King made any effort to do this.

"How are you feeling?" Smith asked.

"Sorry?" Henry said.

"Your brother said you've been off work all week."

"It was nothing. I'm feeling much better now."

Smith guessed his age to be somewhere in the mid to late twenties. His mousy blond hair was thick, and his brown eyes were friendly. His looked to be in good shape and his bare arms were tanned. Smith imagined he could be considered a good-looking man.

"Do you live alone here?" he asked.

"Is it that obvious?"

"Pretty much," Smith said.

"John reckons I'll be a bachelor until the day I die," Henry said. "I've never been one to settle down. What is it you want to know? John told me about the van that was nicked. Why don't you sit down?"

"I'm OK standing up."

"You started the courier company with your brother," DC King said. "Is that right?"

Henry grinned at her. His teeth were white, and it was clear he liked to show them off.

"It was John's brainchild. He'd been following the Covid thing closely ever since it started to spread in China. He predicted that things were about to change, and he reckoned we could cash in on it."

"How did he figure that out?" Smith asked.

"In China everybody was told to stay at home. Only essential workers were allowed out and included in the list of those essential workers were delivery drivers. I told him he was mad in the head. Said it wouldn't be that bad here, but he was right in a way, wasn't he?"

"And you started the courier business?"

"John remortgaged his house and bought six vans," Henry said. "I suggested maybe we should lease, but John reckoned it was better to own our own fleet. At least when we have vans off the road, we're not forced to fork out money every month for them. It paid off. By the end of 2020 we had too much work and we got another five vans. They've paid for themselves. John was able to pay off his mortgage and we're sitting in the pound seats. When will we be able to get the stolen van back?"

"When we're finished with it," Smith said.

"What was wrong with you?" DC King asked.

"Sorry, love?" Henry said.

"Why did you call in sick?" Smith said.

"Stomach bug. I had a dodgy curry."

"And that caused you to miss a week of work?" DC King said.

Henry shrugged his shoulders. "I might have milked it a bit. Our John has always been a bit soft on his little brother."

"Where were you on Thursday?" Smith asked. "Between noon and five?"

"I was at home I think," Henry said.

"Could you think harder?"

"I was here. I might have popped out to the shops, but I was home most of the day."

"Is there anyone who can confirm it?" DC King said.

"Probably not. I live alone."

"What about someone at the shop? Perhaps you paid using a credit card."

"I prefer to use cash," Henry said. "You know where you are with cash."

"What about Friday?" DC King said. "Yesterday morning. Can you tell us what you were doing then?"

"I slept late. I had a bit of a skinful at the pub on Thursday night."

"You were feeling better by then?" Smith said.

Henry smiled. "Must have been. What's this all about? You can't think I had something to do with nicking the van. It belongs to me and John, so why would I want to steal it?"

"When was the last time you were at the depot?" Smith asked.

"Last week sometime," Henry said.

"Could you be more specific?" DC King said.

"Probably Friday. Just over a week ago."

"Do you ever drive the vans?" Smith said.

"Not really."

"I'd appreciate it if you could stick to answering with a simple yes or a no. OK, let's say we were to find something inside that stolen van that can be tied to you – a fingerprint of a piece of your DNA, would you be able to explain how it got there?"

"I've been inside the vans," Henry said. "I've been known to use one to nip down to the shops when it's not needed for work."

"I'm glad we've cleared that up."

"Are you going to explain what this is really about?" Henry said. "I've answered all your questions. I've offered you coffee, which I see you haven't touched – what's going on? This isn't about a stolen van, is it?"

"No," Smith confirmed and left it at that.

"What are you doing here then?"

"Trying to fill in a few blanks," Smith said. "Do you paint?"

"What?"

"Do you like to paint? It's a simple question."

This resulted in a chuckle from Henry. "As a matter of fact, I do."

"I don't see any of your art on the walls," DC King said.

"I don't put my paintings on display," Henry said. "For the simple fact that I'm crap at it."

"Would it be possible to have a look at some of your art?" Smith said.

"No. It's embarrassing."

"What kind of stuff do you like to paint?"

"All sorts."

"What about neo-modernism art?"

"Neo, what?" Henry said.

"Never mind. Do you know a woman by the name of Jennifer Cole?"

"The name doesn't ring a bell."

"What about Davina Hawkins?"

"Nope. Can't say I know anyone by that name."

"We won't take up any more of your time.," Smith said. "Someone will be in touch to inform you when you'll be able to pick up the van. Thanks for the coffee."

"You didn't even drink it."

"Next time maybe," Smith said.

"Will there be a next time?"

"You never can tell, Mr Harvey," Smith said. "You never can tell. We'll see ourselves out."

CHAPTER TWENTY

"I think I'm a bit out of practice, Kerry," Smith said as they drove away from Henry Harvey's house.

"What do you mean by that, Sarge?"

"I'm worried that I might be losing my touch. Am I turning into one of those cliched detectives? The ones who treat everyone like shit even when they know they're not the person they're looking for?"

"No offence, Sarge," DC King said. "But you've always been like that."

"Really?"

"Really," DC King confirmed.

"In that case, I don't feel so bad. The man was an arsehole anyway. Where to next, James?"

"I think you're supposed to tell me, Sarge?"

"In that case, home, James."

"Station?" DC King guessed.

"No," Smith said. "Home. I just need to pop back to my house for something."

For the first time since Smith could remember the dogs didn't pounce on him the moment he set foot inside the house. Instead Theakston and Fred made a beeline for DC King. The old Bull Terrier nuzzled her legs while the hideous Pug seemed content to sit on her feet and drool all over her shoes.

"Sorry about them," Smith said. "No manners."

"It's alright," DC King said. "I love dogs. What are we doing here?"

"I need some decent coffee, and I'm hoping Lucy and Darren are here."

"What are you doing home?" Lucy asked from halfway up the staircase.

"I need your boyfriend's expertise," Smith told her.

"I'll go and wake him up."

"Wake him up?" DC King said. "It's one in the afternoon."

"He's a teenage father," Smith explained.

Darren Lewis came down with Lucy a few minutes later. Smith had made some coffee and he and DC King were sitting at the table in the kitchen. Smith's laptop was busy warming up in front of him.

"Sorry to wake you," he said.

Darren rubbed his eyes. "It's OK. I didn't sleep much last night. Andy kept me up. I think he's got some more teeth coming through."

"When does that actually stop?" Lucy said.

"How old is he?" DC King asked.

"He's a year old."

"Then you've probably got another year of it, but don't worry – the worst is over."

"How come you know so much about this?" Smith said.

"Little brother," DC King said. "Our Dave is eight years younger than me, and I remember it well."

"Lucy said you need my help," Darren said.

Smith opened his emails. "It's a long shot, but I want you to take a look at an email. Don't worry about the mail itself – I want to know if it's possible to trace the sender from the address."

Darren sat down, took one look at the email Smith was pointing at and shook his head.

"Are you sure?" Smith said.

"It's an AFP," Darren said. "An Anonymity Focused Provider. It will almost definitely be encrypted."

"There must be a way to trace it back to the sender."

"If you've got a few years and a lot of high-tech equipment, maybe," Darren said. "This is probably a provider located somewhere like Columbia or

Nigeria. You won't be able to track the sender."

Smith took a sip of coffee. "How did they even get my email address?"

"Which address is it?" Darren asked.

"My personal email."

"Probably from social media. Is your email address on your Facebook profile?"

"I have no idea."

Darren shook his head. "Open your Facebook."

Smith did so. "Now what?"

"Give it here."

Darren tapped the keypad and opened the settings.

"You've included your email address. And your security settings are non-existent."

"Why would I need security settings?" Smith asked.

"Because this is open for anyone to see."

"Who cares? I have nine friends – three of those are now deceased, and I haven't posted anything since Erica forced me to post a photo of Andrew nine months ago."

"It means that anyone who knows your name can get hold of your email address, Sarge," DC King informed him.

After another few taps on the keypad Darren told Smith his profile could only be viewed by people in his friends list.

"All six of them," Smith said. "Unless there's a special setting that allows the people who have expired to take a look from beyond the grave."

"I thought he was just like this at work," DC King dared.

"Nope," Lucy said. "He's like it all the time. You should try living with him."

"I can imagine."

"I am still in the room," Smith reminded them. "Where's Laura?"

"Next door with Fran," Darren said.

"Those two are inseparable these days," Smith said. "I suppose we'd better get back to do some work."

The unmistakable wails of Andrew could be heard from upstairs.

"Definitely time to get out of here," Smith decided.

"I'll go and see to Andrew," Lucy said. "Darren was up all night with him."

"I'll see you later," Smith said. "I don't know what time we'll be back."

"Aren't you going to shut your laptop down?" Darren asked.

"Can you do it for me?"

"OK. You've received a new email."

Darren's facial expression was one of utter bewilderment. Smith snatched the laptop away from him and read the screen.

You're not looking hard enough, Detective Smith.
You could have saved her if you'd paid more attention.
It appears I overestimated you, so I'll give you some more help.
Look more closely at the paintings.
Perhaps my next subject will get to live if you do.

CHAPTER TWENTY ONE

"It was signed *The Painter* again," Smith told the team. He'd grabbed his laptop before it had even shut down and headed straight to the station. Darren Lewis had been told in no uncertain terms that he would be sleeping on the streets if he breathed so much as one word of what he'd read in the email. Smith got the impression the teenager had taken him seriously.

"What exactly is it we're supposed to be looking for?" Whitton said.

"Look more closely at the paintings," Smith repeated what had been said in the email. "That's what we need to focus all our attention on. There is something in them we've missed. I did a bit of digging last night, and there are some slight differences between the painting in the background at Jennifer Cole's house. Some more Roman numerals have been painted on, and they were painted in Jennifer's blood. Can we link this up to the big screen?"

He tapped his laptop.

Three minutes later the team were looking at the two images on the screen. Arno Barnard's *Maze of Chaos* was on the left and next to it was *The Painter*'s version. Smith got up and tapped the part of the painting that differed from the original.

"Can we enhance this bit?"

DC Moore did his best.

"How can this be related to the murder?" Bridge said. "It's just a load of Roman numerals. What has it got to do with Jennifer Cole?"

"We're looking at this the wrong way," DC King said.

"What are you thinking, Kerry?" Smith said.

"If we analyse the wording in the email," DC King said. "The person who calls himself *The Painter* isn't referring to the victim found with the painting

– he's talking about his next victim."

"Of course," Smith said. "I need some more sleep. It would be impossible to prevent the murder of someone he's already killed, but he's telling me there's a clue about his next victim in the painting of the one before."

"If that's the case," DC Moore said. "There is something in those Roman numerals that relates to Davina Hawkins."

"What though?" Bridge said.

DI Smyth came inside the room and took a seat next to Smith.

"Good meeting, boss?" Smith asked.

"No," DI Smyth said. "What have I missed?"

Smith told him about the most recent email and what they believed *The Painter* was hinting at.

DI Smyth looked closely at the highlighted Roman numerals and frowned.

"Why did he paint them like that?"

"Like what?" Smith said.

"At an angle. Some of them aren't straight."

"Half of the numerals in the original painting aren't straight either," Whitton pointed out.

"No," DI Smyth said. "The ones in the original *Maze of Chaos* are random – the ones *The Painter* added on follow a certain pattern."

"What does it mean though?" Smith said.

"Does someone have a piece of paper?" DI Smyth said.

DC King handed him one. DI Smyth took out a pen and started to write.

"I'm a bit rusty," he said. "So, we might need to double check this, but the numerals running across the page are the number one, and the number eight-hundred. I and DCCC."

"That's correct, sir," DC Moore held out his phone.

DI Smyth tilted his head. "LIII. Fifty-three. And IXDC is nine thousand…"

"Six hundred, sir," DC Moore confirmed. "Nine thousand, six hundred."

"Any thoughts?" Smith said.

The silence that followed told him that nobody had any idea what the Roman numerals could mean.

"Perhaps it's a phone number," DC King suggested eventually.

"1800," Smith said. "And 539600. That doesn't sound like any phone number I've ever seen."

"What was the number of the house Davina lived at?" DC Moore said.

"Sixteen," Smith said. "16 Garden Street."

"No connection there then," Whitton decided.

"It's possible we're barking up the wrong tree," Bridge said. "Maybe the Roman numerals are not what we're supposed to be looking at."

"No," Smith said. "They're exactly what we need to look at. He added those numerals for a reason."

"Can I say something?" It was DC Moore.

"Harry?" DI Smyth said.

"Why are we wasting all this time trying to decipher a puzzle when the woman who it's pointing towards is already dead? We're too late to save her anyway."

Smith glared at him. "This isn't about saving Davina Hawkins, you idiot. This is about figuring out the killer's cryptic message and maybe standing a chance of stopping him from butchering another woman. Have you got that?"

"Sorry, Sarge," DC Moore said. "I just thought…"

"Well stop thinking," Smith interrupted. "And do me a favour, stop talking too. You're not helping."

DC Moore raised his hands in apology but remained silent.

"Clear the screen," DI Smyth said.

DC Moore tapped the keypad of the laptop, and the screen became blank. DI Smyth walked up to it and wrote the numbers on it as they appeared in the painting. Then he wrote them again side by side.

"Damn it," he said. "What are we supposed to be looking at?"

"It has to mean something," Smith said.

"All I see is a load of random numbers," Whitton said.

"What about their corresponding letters," DC King suggested.

"1800," DI Smyth said. "AHOO."

He wrote this on the board.

"53," he read. "EC. 9600 – IEOO. That's not it."

They were stopped from analysing it further when someone came inside the room. It was PC Griffin.

"We're busy," Smith told him.

"Sorry to interrupt," the beak-nosed PC said. "But we might have a hit from one of the neighbours of Davina Hawkins. Their CCTV camera picked up a courier van in the road around the time of the murder, and the footage is pretty clear."

"We'll look into it later," Smith said. "We're in the middle of something here."

PC Griffin looked at the screen at the back of the room.

"Will that be all?" DI Smyth said.

"Where is that?" PC Griffin pointed to the screen.

"What?" Smith said.

"The GPS coordinates," PC Griffin said. "Where is that? It's somewhere close to the Minster, isn't it?"

Smith looked at him and then he turned to look at DI Smyth.

"GPS coordinates," he said.

"You get so used to them these days, don't you?" PC Griffin said. "We start to recognise certain ones."

"Harry," DI Smyth said.

DC Moore held up his phone. "Already on it, sir."

Time seemed to slow down in the small conference room. All eyes were on DC Moore as he typed the coordinates into the GPS on his phone. "Got it," he said after a while. "53.9600 north – 1.0800 west. You'll never guess where that is."

"16 Garden Street," Smith said.

CHAPTER TWENTY TWO

The euphoria the team experienced in the small conference room was short lived. No matter how closely they examined the painting found at the scene of Davina Hawkins' murder they couldn't find anything resembling GPS coordinates in the body of the canvas.

This was explained quite quickly though, and the person responsible for shedding light on the mystery was Grant Webber. The Head of Forensics came there in person to show them what his team had found, and now everyone inside the room was looking at the image of the woman's face on the large screen.

"That's really creepy," DC King said. "If that's the face of his next victim, it's creepy as hell."

"How did he even do it?" Smith wondered. "The fingerprint in the painting was tiny. How did he even paint it, let alone add a face into it?"

"He didn't," Webber said. "He made it look like he did. That's why it's taken me so long to bring this to you. We've spent all afternoon comparing the photographs of the victim's body with the painting he did of her body, and the smudge on her right thigh is simply that – a smudge of blood. But what appears to be a replication of that smudge is, in fact an incredibly detailed transfer of a woman's face. Possibly taken from a photograph of her. Technology has come a long way, and it is now possible to transfer a photo of anything onto any surface. In this instance the image in the transfer was extremely intricate, and not visible to the naked eye."

"And he transferred it to the painting," Smith said.

"That's precisely what he did."

"Bloody hell," Bridge commented.

"What are we supposed to do with this information?" DC Moore said. "It's not like we can broadcast the woman's face and ask anyone matching her description to be extremely careful of any portrait artists who come across as being a bit dodgy."

"That's exactly what we need to do," Smith said.

"The woman in question has very unusual features," Webber said. "She has a face that is not likely to be forgotten."

"That ought to work in our favour," Smith said.

"This is the most insane idea you've ever had," DC Moore said.

"Do you have any better ones? If we're right about this, another woman is going to die. Another woman is going to be slaughtered, and we're going to have another painting to decipher. I don't know about the rest of you, but I'm already sick and tired of this psychopath. This is a way to stop him."

"It's risky," DI Smyth said. "We put this face out there, we're going to create mass panic. Everyone who knows a woman who even vaguely resembles her is going to be calling in."

"A woman is going to be killed if we don't, boss." Smith was adamant. "I'll speak to PC Walker myself."

"I agree with DS Smith," DC King said. "And the press liaison officer ought to know the best way to proceed with it."

"Alright," DI Smyth decided. "We'll risk it. But I'll be the one to liaise with PC Walker. We need to tread extremely carefully with this."

"We've managed to confirm that the painting found at the first victim's house was painted in stages," Webber said. "The background was done some time before the portrait of the woman."

"How much time are we talking?" Smith asked.

"At least a week, possibly two. When we scraped away the outer layer, the paint underneath was old. And the material used was water-based paint. The victim's portrait was completed in oil-based paint."

"He's been in their houses," Smith said. "The bastard has been inside the victims' houses."

"It's the only explanation," Webber agreed. "He must have somehow gained access, and that's how he knew about the fireplace and the painting above it in the first victim's place."

"What about Davina Hawkins?" Smith said. "Was that painting done over time too?"

"Yes and no. I believe the outline was done beforehand, but he completed the majority of the painting at the scene."

"She was left on display," DC King said. "Naked and sprawled on a chair."

"And that's how she was painted," Smith said. "Which means he planned to leave her like that all along. If her outline was painted beforehand, he knew exactly how he was going to put her on display."

"What can you tell us about the van?" DI Smyth said.

"It is definitely the vehicle your painter used to travel to the scenes of the two murders," Webber confirmed. "The blood on the driver's seat came from victim number one, and the paint on the steering wheel matched the paint used on the portrait of victim number two. That's all I have for you at this stage."

"Thanks, Webber," DI Smyth said. "I suggest we all take a short break. We've been at it all day, and I for one am feeling it."

Smith had no objections there. It had been a while since he'd been able to smoke a cigarette and he needed to do something about that. He left the room and headed for the exit. He was met in the corridor by PC Griffin.

"Good work back there," he managed.

"Sarge?" PC Griffin said.

"You connected the numbers to GPS coordinates," Smith said. "Well spotted."

"I would have thought it was obvious."

"No, it wasn't."

"It was to me."

"What is your problem?" Smith said. "When a superior officer hands out a compliment, you're supposed to accept it."

"I suppose it depends on who the superior officer is," PC Griffin said. He paused and added, "Sarge."

Smith debated whether to carry on the discussion but decided against it. He really wasn't in the mood for PC Griffin right now. He walked past him and opened the door.

The late afternoon sun felt good on his face. Smith lit a cigarette and took a long drag. The door to the station opened and DCI Chalmers came outside. He walked over to Smith and lit his own cigarette.

"Afternoon, boss," Smith said. "Beautiful day."

"It is now," Chalmers said. "I'm about to knock off for the day."

"The benefits of being at the top of the food chain."

"Not bloody likely. It's Saturday in case you've forgotten. I only got dragged in on the weekend because old Smyth decided to show his face on a weekend for a change. The man is seriously doing my head in."

"What's Uncle Jeremy done now?" Smith asked.

"The public-school amoeba is talking about a special general meeting to discuss the way forward in the wake of the pandemic. What the hell for? I'm not the only one who would prefer to forget all about it. It's over – end of story."

Smith laughed. "He does like his meetings."

"Where are we with *The Painter* thing?" Chalmers said.

"I thought the DI had brought you up to date with that. Didn't you have a briefing?"

"We were supposed to, but old Smyth steered it in the direction he wanted it to go. The Super isn't interested in murder investigations. As long as we crack them, that's all he gives a shit about. Talk to me."

"He's been sending me emails," Smith said. "Telling me I'm not looking closely enough at what's right in front of my face. The bastard is taunting me."

"Don't take it so personally."

"He sent the emails to my personal email address," Smith said. "How else am I supposed to take it?"

"What else do we know?"

"Not enough. We figured out something from the first painting. There was another painting in the background, and he added some Roman numerals to it. Those numerals corresponded to the GPS coordinates for the address of the second victim. And in the portrait of that murder scene there was a transfer of a woman's face. I think that's his next intended victim, and I suggested we put it out there for the whole city to see."

"Be very careful."

"That's exactly what the DI said," Smith told him. "It's risky – I know it is, but I don't know what else we can do."

Chalmers stubbed out his cigarette and patted Smith on the shoulder. "I'd better be off. I promised Mrs Chalmers I'd take her shopping before the shops close."

"How is she?" Smith said.

"Almost back to normal. The docs are positive she'll be back to her old self very soon, and that's what I'm worried about."

"You don't mean that."

"I bloody well do. Keep me up to date."

"Will do, boss," Smith said.

He put out his cigarette and was about to light another when Whitton came outside.

"I thought I'd find you out here," she said. "We've got a lead."

"I like the sound of that," Smith said.

"One of the prints found in the abandoned van sounded a few warning bells. It's in the system."

"Who is it?"

"A man by the name of Brian Lloyd."

"It doesn't ring a bell."

"He's spent more time inside than he has out of it," Whitton said.

"Brian Lloyd. Nope, never heard of him."

"He did eighteen months for assault a couple of years ago," Whitton said.

"Assault is a far cry from multiple murder," Smith pointed out.

"The victim was a woman. And according to the records he got off lightly. It should have been attempted murder, but he was able to afford a fancy lawyer and they failed to prove that his intent was to kill her."

CHAPTER TWENTY THREE

It was late by the time Brian Lloyd had been booked in and ready to be interviewed. He hadn't put up much of a fight when he was apprehended in the pub in Heslington, and he'd made the call to his lawyer in the back of the police car on the way to the station.

Smith didn't think he was *The Painter*. He had an impressive record. He'd been in and out of jail since the age of eighteen, but his crimes were a far cry from the recent brutal murders. Smith voiced these concerns with DI Smyth prior to the interview.

"You always say that," DI Smyth reminded him. "You always say he's not our guy."

"And I'm usually right," Smith pointed out. "Brian Lloyd is a nasty piece of work and an all-round scumbag, but the actions of *The Painter* display a certain amount of sophistication. Brian Lloyd doesn't fit the bill."

"We can't ignore the fact that his prints were inside that van."

"What has he got to say about that?" Smith said.

"He's refused to say anything," DI Smyth said. "Which is his right."

"It's not him."

"We'll reserve judgement on that until after we've spoken to him, shall we?"

"What did PC Walker think of the public appeal with the woman's face?" Smith said.

"He suggested we don't divulge the reason her face is being broadcast to the world."

"How is that going to work?"

"A missing person."

"Don't we need a name for that?" Smith said.

"Usually, but as we don't have one, we'll have to improvise. PC Walker suggested we keep it vague. The police are looking for anyone who might have seen the woman to get in touch."

"What time is it going out?"

"It's already out there," DI Smyth said. "Hopefully someone will know who she is."

"I'm just going out for a quick smoke," Smith said.

"You've got five minutes."

The sun had said its goodbyes to the city for another day and the air was chillier than it had been. Smith lit a cigarette and typed a quick message to Whitton. He told her he didn't expect to be long. Brian Lloyd wasn't *The Painter*, and Smith was sure that would be made very clear in the interview.

His phone beeped to tell him he'd received a message, and he assumed it was Whitton replying to his. When he swiped the screen, he realised he was half right. It was Whitton, but she was telling him he'd received another email from the person they believed to be *The Painter*. Smith had asked her to keep an eye on his emails. He didn't feel like playing a game of WhatsApp ping pong, so he phoned her.

"What did he say?" he asked.

"He must have seen the appeal for the woman," Whitton said.

"Could you read out the email?"

"Bravo, Detective Smith," Whitton read. "Perhaps I didn't afford you the credit you deserve. But you will have to act with a bit more haste with the next one."

"Fuck."

"Jason?"

"She's already dead, isn't she?"

"We don't know that," Whitton said.

"What else could that email mean? You'll have to act with a bit more haste with the next one? She's dead. We're too late. When did the email arrive?"

"Just before I sent you the message," Whitton said.

"We're about to interview a suspect who had nothing to do with those murders, Erica. Brian Lloyd had his phone taken away from him when he was booked in. We're wasting time."

"It's late," Whitton said. "There's nothing we can do now."

"Another woman is already dead. Somewhere in this city is a dead woman holding the key to who the next dead woman is going to be, and we don't have a fucking clue."

"You need to calm down."

"I am calm," Smith insisted. "I'd better go. I'll see you later."

He went back inside the station and told DI Smyth about the email.

"You know what this means, don't you?"

"Brian Lloyd is not *The Painter*."

"Not only that," Smith said. "The woman whose face is out there for the entire city to see is already dead."

"We don't know that."

"She's dead."

"He could be bluffing," DI Smyth said. "It's possible he didn't expect us to find the transfer of the face so quickly, and the public appeal has got him rattled. It is very possible the woman is still alive."

"I hope so. Are we still going to bother interviewing Lloyd?"

"It needs to be done. His fingerprints were found in a van we believe was involved in two murders. He needs to be interviewed."

It was probably the shortest interview Smith had ever been involved in. Brian Lloyd's legal representative had advised him to answer any questions put to him and the notorious criminal had admitted to being inside the van. He'd seen it abandoned in the stretch of open ground and taken the opportunity to see if there was anything he could help himself to. The doors of the van were unlocked, and his fingerprints ended up there when he removed the satellite navigation system. The Satnav in question was in a box in his garage if they needed proof.

    Smith believed him. He didn't need proof – he knew Brian Lloyd was telling the truth. He was a hardened criminal, but he wasn't *The Painter*. The theft of the Satnav was a minor offence but as Brian was still on license, it was likely he would be heading back to prison. Smith really didn't care one way or the other. He had much bigger fish to fry than Brian Lloyd.

CHAPTER TWENTY FOUR

While Smith and DI Smyth were chasing the wild goose that was Brian Lloyd, Bridge and DC Moore were taking a look at the CCTV footage that PC Griffin had brought to their attention.

"We dropped the ball there with the GPS coordinates, didn't we?" Bridge said. "It took a rookie PC seconds to spot what we'd been working on for hours."

"We did all the leg work for him," DC Moore said. "And sometimes a fresh pair of eyes is all it takes."

"I suppose you're right."

"Perhaps we should bring him onto the team."

"Smith would love that."

"Smith is not the only detective in this station," DC Moore reminded him.

"Smith is his own worst enemy sometimes."

"Well I don't appreciate being spoken to like that. I'm not an idiot."

"He didn't mean it," Bridge said. "Smith has always taken things far too personally. He gets too involved and he interprets every murder as a personal attack on himself. It's what makes him such an asset to the team."

"Or a hindrance."

"He won't change," Bridge said. "You will never change Jason Smith."

DC Moore inserted the USB containing the camera footage and started it from the beginning.

"This makes a nice change," Bridge said. "You can actually make out what's on the footage for once."

The CCTV camera was attached to a house on the opposite side of the road to Davina Hawkins' house. The footage was extremely clear. It captured a wide-angle view of numbers 16 and 18 Garden Street as well as the road in front. The time at the bottom of the screen was: 08:38.

"Can you speed it up a bit?" Bridge asked. "I don't feel like spending all night looking at this screen."

DC Moore selected the option that replayed the footage at three times the normal speed, and they watched the screen carefully.

"There," Bridge said at 09:32.

DC Moore paused the file. A dark-coloured van had arrived on the road. It slowed down and came to a stop outside Davina Hawkins' house. DC Moore zoomed in on it.

"Gotcha."

The decals on the side told them it was the stolen Harvey's Couriers van.

Nothing happened for a few minutes, then someone appeared from the side of the screen. It looked like an elderly woman, and she was walking slowly. The clock on the screen told them it took her over two minutes to cover a distance of only fifty metres.

"I wonder if she saw who was inside the van," Bridge said.

"I doubt it," DC Moore said. "The windows are tinted."

Another two minutes passed and the driver side door of the van opened. DC Moore slowed down the footage and they watched it frame by frame. A figure emerged from the van then suddenly disappeared.

"Where has he gone?" DC Moore said.

"Keep watching," Bridge said.

"There he is," DC Moore said a minute later.

The person on the screen had his back to the camera and they couldn't make out his face.

"Shit," Bridge said. "You can't even see if it's a man or a woman."

"It's a bloke," DC Moore decided. "And he's carrying something."

They watched him walk up the path towards the door of number 16. A hand was raised to ring the bell and shortly afterwards the door opened.

What occurred next happened very quickly. The door was forced open wider, and the van driver was inside the house in an instant. Then the door closed again.

"It's definitely The *Painter*," Bridge decided.

"Hopefully we'll get a better shot of him when he comes out again," DC Moore said. "Shall I speed it up again?"

The time on the screen was now 09:44.

People came and went. Cars moved off and other cars parked on the road, but the door to number 16 remained closed. At 11:15 DC Moore thought he'd spotted something moving inside the house, but when he rewound the footage and watched it again, he realised it was just the living room curtains blowing in the breeze.

"Perhaps we should go back," Bridge suggested. "To when he entered the house."

"What for?" DC Moore asked.

"We've been focusing on the front door. Maybe we should keep an eye on the living room window. We might see what's happening inside the house."

"The curtains are obscuring the view," DC Moore said. "He should be coming back out soon. The fiancé got back just before 12 so he will be nearly finished in there."

Nothing else happened for a while but at 11:50 there was movement next to the van. The door opened and someone climbed inside.

"What the hell?" Bridge said. "Did we miss something?"

DC Moore rewound the footage, and they focused their eyes on the front door. *The Painter* didn't come back out.

"The bastard went round the back," Bridge said.

"Do you think he knew about the camera?" DC Moore said. "He made his getaway round the back and then crouched down beneath the parked cars."

"It's looking that way. "What's happening there?"

They watched as the van sped away from the kerb then came to a dead stop. There was a man in the middle of the road. The CCTV camera caught him looking up from his phone and raising his hands. He crossed over the road and the van disappeared out of the shot.

"Damn it," Bridge said. "That was the fiancé. If only he'd been a few minutes earlier he would have caught *The Painter* in the act."

Later, Lionel Grange would watch the CCTV footage and come to the same conclusion. It would dawn on him that had he not acted so spontaneously at the travel agent and booked the holiday to Thailand it was possible Davina Hawkins might still be alive.

CHAPTER TWENTY FIVE

Smith thanked DI Smyth for the lift and asked him if he wanted to come in for a drink.

"I'd better get home," he said. "It's been a hell of a day. I need some sleep and I suggest you get some too."

"Not going to happen, boss," Smith said. "Not while there's a dead woman somewhere out there with a clue to who the next victim is going to be. This bastard is one step ahead of us the whole time, and that tends to keep me awake at night."

"We'll get him. We always get them in the end."

"He knew about the camera. He left Davina Hawkins' house out the back because he knew the CCTV across the road would catch his face."

"Get some sleep," DI Smyth said.

He drove off before Smith could say anything else.

Smith went inside his house and heard the sound of voices in the kitchen. He greeted the dogs and walked down the hallway. Whitton was talking to Sheila Rogers at the kitchen table. There was a half-full bottle of wine in front of them. Smith remembered that he'd run out of beers, but he opened the fridge anyway out of habit. He was pleasantly surprised – the bottom shelf was full of bottles of beer. He took one out and closed the fridge door.

"I got some more on the way home," Whitton explained. "I thought you might need one."

"Have I told you lately how much I love you," Smith said.

He kissed her on the top of the head and sat down.

"Hi, Shelia," he added.

"Hi," she said.

"Sheila popped round to pick up Fran," Whitton said. "But she and Laura are lights out upstairs, so we opened a bottle of wine."

"We don't have any wine," Smith said.

"I went to fetch a bottle when I realised my daughter wasn't going anywhere anytime soon," Shelia said. "Rough day?"

Smith downed his beer. "You could say that."

"I heard about the murders."

"News travels fast."

"You'll catch him though, won't you?" Sheila said. "You always do."

She gave him a smile and Smith reciprocated with a half-smile of his own.

"Where are Lucy and Darren?" he asked Whitton.

"Also sleeping," she said. "You should see them. Lucy, Darren and Andrew all cuddled up on the bed. I took a photo."

Smith helped himself to another beer.

"Did you watch the public appeal?"

"It was on the evening news," Whitton said. "And again, on the later edition. She's a striking looking woman. Someone will know who she is."

"I hope so."

"I see your house is on the market," Whitton said to Sheila.

"It came as quite a shock," Sheila said. "The landlord didn't even warn me about it. I got a phone call, and the next thing I know the estate agent is on my doorstep telling me he needs to come in to take some photographs. I wasn't even consulted."

"That's landlords for you," Smith said. "You should be given first option to buy."

"I wish. I won't get a mortgage based on what I get paid at the school. I can barely make ends meet as it is, and my bastard of an ex isn't helping. He's behind on his payments. I've put my solicitor onto him, but so far, I haven't heard anything."

"I'm so sorry," Whitton said.

"Can I use your bathroom?" Sheila asked.

"Of course," Whitton said. "You know where it is."

She left the kitchen and Smith sighed deeply.

"We'll find her," Whitton said. "We'll find the woman in the transfer."

She rested her head on his shoulder.

"You know that when we do, she'll already be dead?" Smith said. "You know that don't you? And we'll have another fucking painting to try and decipher. Why is he doing this, Erica? How can he get off on slaughtering women and painting them?"

"We'll find out. It's still early days."

"Three women are dead. And I've got a feeling this one isn't going to stop until we catch him. We have two bodies and nothing to show for it. How is that even possible?"

"These things take time," Whitton said. "There are only so many hours in the day."

"We don't have time with this one, Erica. Time is running out for another woman and very soon I'm going to receive another email from that sick bastard. Shit…"

"What's wrong?"

"I left my laptop at work," Smith said. "With everything that was going on I forgot to pick it up. What if he's already sent me an email? What if he's going to give us another clue. I need to go back and get the laptop."

He tried to get to his feet but Whitton's hand on his shoulder stopped him.

"Relax. You can check your emails on your phone."

Smith nodded and sighed deeply. He swiped the screen of his phone and opened his emails.

"Nothing."

"There you go then," Whitton said. "Drink your beer."

Smith obliged. "I can't get that woman's face out of my head. We have no idea who she is, but she's almost certainly dead."

His phoned beeped and he almost dropped his beer. He dared to look at the screen and saw that it was a message from DI Smyth. Sheila Roberts came back inside the kitchen.

"I can go if you want to talk shop."

"There's no need for that," Whitton told her. "Shop talk can wait until tomorrow."

She poured them both another glass of wine.

"I need to make a phone call," Smith said. "I'll go out and have a smoke."

The message from DI Smyth was asking whether he was available to talk. Smith wondered why he'd even bothered to ask – he didn't usually. He closed the back door and lit a cigarette. He brought up DI Smyth's number and took a long drag of the cigarette.

"Sorry to bother you at home," DI Smyth said when he answered.

"Go on," Smith urged.

"The tech team have finished with Jennifer Cole's mobile phone."

"What took them so long?" Smith asked.

"They did a thorough audit of all incoming and outgoing correspondence," DI Smyth explained. "Including deleted messages. It was those ones that took a bit longer to retrieve. You know how it goes."

Smith did. "Service providers and all that crap. Did they find something?"

"They did. Miss Cole sent a message to a number not in her contact list on Saturday last week."

"That was four days before she was killed," Smith calculated.

"Her message was answered almost immediately," DI Smyth said. "And a thread of messages followed."

"And?"

"It appears she replied to an advert for portrait painting. I've asked the tech team to compile a detailed printout of the entire message thread, but I'll give you the gist of it now. Jennifer replied to the number on the advert enquiring about the cost and the ins and outs. She was told the portrait would be done at a place of her choosing, and if she wasn't satisfied, she was under no obligation to pay."

Smith's cigarette had gone out. He lit it again and took a long drag.

"Are you still there?" DI Smyth asked.

"Still here, boss," Smith said. "That's how he gets them where he wants them. He creates a false sense of security by making them believe they're in control of the location, and the no obligation to pay thing draws them further in. I don't think Jennifer Cole is the only woman he's tried this on."

"I'm not following you."

"I think there will have been more," Smith said. "Women more suspicious than Jennifer. All he has to do is admit defeat and move on. He will only choose the ones he believes he's fooled. What else do we know?"

"I've got bad news," DI Smyth said.

"The phone number he uses doesn't exist anymore," Smith guessed.

"Correct. Probably pay-as-you-go, and the sim is no longer in use."

"We need to find out where she saw the advert."

"We do," DI Smyth agreed. "It gives us something else to look at."

"Why did she delete the messages?" Smith wondered.

"Excuse me?" DI Smyth said.

"Why delete the messages? They're hardly anything to be ashamed of."

"Perhaps she liked to keep a clean house where her phone is concerned. I don't think it's important."

"Do we know if she deleted any other messages?"

"The woman from the tech team didn't mention anything."

"I think he did it," Smith decided. "I think he knew we would find them, and he deleted them to make it harder for us."

"That's not important. We'll speak to Jennifer's girlfriend again tomorrow. Perhaps she mentioned something about having her portrait painted. Enjoy what's left of your evening."

Sheila Rogers had gone when Smith went back inside.

"She told me to say goodbye," Whitton said. "What did the DI want?"

Smith told her about the deleted messages on Jennifer Cole's phone.

"That's how he does it. He advertises portrait painting, and that's how he manages to gain access to their houses."

"Davina Hawkins didn't seem to want him inside her house," Whitton reminded him. "The CCTV footage showed her trying to fight him off when he tried to get inside."

"Perhaps she didn't like what she saw," Smith suggested. "Perhaps she realised something wasn't right. This is how he does it, Erica. And I get the feeling that this is how we're going to catch him."

CHAPTER TWENTY SIX

Smith was feeling more positive than he had been since the beginning of the investigation. Even the phone call from Gary Lewis informing him about the fate of his car hadn't dampened his spirits. Darren's brother had called to give him the bad news about his trusty Ford Sierra early the next morning. In Gary's opinion the car wasn't worth fixing. There were just too many things wrong with it, and the cost of repairs would come to more than double what the car was actually worth.

"Are you alright?" Whitton asked when he'd broken the news to her.
"I suppose this day was bound to come around sooner or later," Smith said.
"I know how much you loved that car," Whitton said. "Even though it's been off the road more than it's been on it recently."
"It is what it is."
"We can look for another car when things quieten down a bit."
"What for?"
"Because the death of the Sierra means you'll be without a car."
"I'm starting to like being driven around," Smith said. "There's no rush to replace the old Ford. Can I catch a lift with you to work?"

He was still in high spirits when they arrived at the station. It was a glorious July day, and he was confident they were going to get a step closer to *The Painter* today. He checked his emails and saw there were no new messages from the killer. He wondered if this meant he was finished. He picked up some coffee from the machine in the canteen and took it with him to the small conference room.

The smile was wiped from his face in an instant when Smith saw who was sitting at the table. PC Griffin was leaning back in the chair, grinning like he belonged there.

Smith remained standing. "What are you doing here?"

"I've been temporarily assigned to the team," PC Griffin said.

"Over my dead body."

"I was as surprised as you clearly are. But who am I to disobey a direct order?"

"Who's idea was this?" Smith asked.

"I was just told to report to DI Smyth. I believe it's he who is leading this investigation."

Smith nodded and left the room.

He found DI Smyth inside his office.

"What the hell were you thinking?"

"I presume PC Griffin has made his presence known?" DI Smyth said.

"I can't work with the man."

"You will work with whoever you're told to work with, Smith. The team could benefit from a fresh pair of eyes."

"There are plenty of other pairs of eyes you could have chosen," Smith argued. "What about Baldwin? She's worked more murder cases than I can remember."

"PC Baldwin is otherwise engaged."

"I don't want Griffin on the team, boss."

"You seem to forget who gave us the break with the GPS coordinates. PC Griffin may be an objectionable human being, but he's astute, and it's clear that he's keen to learn. I believe he will be an asset to the team, and his assignment is only temporary."

"Do I have any say in this?" Smith said.

"None whatsoever. I won't be pairing the two of you off – I'm not suicidal, but you will be expected to work alongside him in a professional manner. Understood?"

"Loud and clear, boss. I used to like you."

"Good to hear it. Now we've cleared that up, how about we see if we can catch a serial killer."

DI Smyth outlined the progress made in the investigation thus far for the benefit of PC Griffin and the beak-nosed constable listened without interrupting. When DI Smyth was finished, he asked if he had any questions and PC Griffin told him he didn't. Smith was glad. He was keen to get started, and he didn't want to get held up.

"There is one thing I don't understand," PC Griffin said.
Smith's groan was so loud everybody in the room turned to look in his direction.
"Go on," DI Smyth said.
"I'm not doubting the competency of the team," PC Griffin said. "It appears you've already covered much more than I thought would be possible in the time you've had, but have you considered art colleges and students at the university who are studying art? From what I've seen the person you've dubbed *The Painter* is an exceptional artist. It's possible he or she has received a high level of training."
"We've considered it," Smith told him. "And you're right about the talent on display, but from a logistical perspective there simply are not enough hours in the day to undertake something like that. The students at the university and the colleges are on their summer break, and the majority of the faculty will be away too, and it's just not possible to carry out such a mammoth task."
"It would have been the first thing I looked into."
"I probably would have thought the same," Smith said. "When I first arrived at CID, but I soon came to understand how things worked in this department. Perhaps you'll learn to appreciate it when you have a bit more experience under your belt."
"I just thought..."

"DS Smith is right," DI Smyth cut PC Griffin short. "Moving on. We now know that Jennifer Price was in contact with someone claiming to offer portrait painting. A number of messages on her phone confirms it. It's possible Jennifer's girlfriend was aware of it and we'll be speaking to her again this morning."

"The message thread was deleted," Smith said. "I think *The Painter* was the one who deleted the messages."

"Why?" It was PC Griffin.

"To buy him some time," DC King said. "It takes quite a while to retrieve deleted messages."

Smith gave her an appreciative smile.

"We had a positive response to the public appeal yesterday," DI Smyth continued. "And a team is sifting through the calls that came in. The woman on the transfer has a face that is not easily forgotten, and I'm positive we'll know who she is during the course of the day. It's possible we're too late, but we have to work on the assumption that we're not."

"She's dead," Smith said. "The wording in the last email left little doubt about that, but there will be a painting that gives us a clue about the next victim when we find her."

The door to the room opened and PC Baldwin came inside.

"Sorry to interrupt. I've been working through the calls that came in after the public appeal and I think we have two positive leads to look into."

Smith realised that's what DI Smyth meant when he mentioned that Baldwin was *otherwise engaged*.

"A lecturer at the university called in," she said. "She was in the same year as a woman matching the description of the one we put out. She claims to have spoken to the woman yesterday. And a man out walking his dog is convinced he saw her in Heslington."

"How reliable are these witnesses?" PC Griffin asked.

"They've volunteered to come in," Baldwin said. "I got the impression they were genuine."

"That's good enough for me," Smith told her.

"I'll let you know when they arrive. They've promised to get here as soon as they can."

"Thanks, Baldwin."

"Right," DI Smyth said. "Smith, you seem keen to go and speak to Jennifer Cole's girlfriend. Kerry, you can go with him. Bridge, I want you and Harry to talk to the fiancé of the second victim. Take the footage of the CCTV from Friday morning with you and ask him to watch it."

"That's a bit rough, isn't it?" DC Moore said.

"It is, but it might jog a few memories. Whitton, you and I are going to stick around for when the potential witnesses get here. I want someone to speak to them as soon as they arrive."

"What about me?" PC Griffin said.

"It seems we've got everything covered for now," DI Smyth said. "Your assignment here is generally on a watch-and-learn basis, so to begin with you can do just that. Take a break – grab a cup of coffee."

"Would you mind if I did a bit of research on local artists while I'm twiddling my thumbs?"

"By all means. We'll have another briefing later this afternoon."

CHAPTER TWENTY SEVEN

"What was the DI thinking when he brought PC Griffin onto the team?" DC King said.
"The term *fresh pair of eyes* was mentioned," Smith said. "He could be right."
"I thought you hated PC Griffin."
"That hasn't changed. At least the boss has made sure he understands what his role on the team is."
 "A friend of mine is selling his car," DC King said out of the blue.
"Great." Smith didn't know what else to say.
"It's a 2015 Ford Fiesta, and it's going for a great price."
"Why are you telling me this, Kerry?"
"I thought you were on the lookout for a new car."
"You thought wrong," Smith said.
"Whitton said the Sierra had finally been declared deceased. Her words."
"And you thought I'd be considering replacing it already?" Smith said. "I haven't even had time to mourn."
"You're a really strange man, Sarge."
"Don't you forget it."
 The smell of the paint was still apparent when Patti Apple opened the door of number 45 Highfield Avenue. The tang of the oil-based paint wasn't as strong as it had been when Smith was there a few days ago but it still lingered.
"You'd better come in," Patti said.
She stepped to the side and Smith and DC King went inside the house.
 She didn't invite them into the living room, and Smith understood why. The scene in there was still fresh inside his own head, and he couldn't imagine how Patti Apple must feel about it. He was surprised she'd gone

back to the house so soon. They sat in the kitchen. Patti offered them coffee and Smith accepted the offer. He asked his first questions while Patti was busy making it.

"Can you remember Jennifer ever mentioning anything about having her portrait painted?"

Patti poured some water into the kettle, and switched it on.

"Her portrait?"

"Did she ever talk about getting one done?" DC King said.

"I suggested she should, but she never seemed to take it seriously."

"There is a possibility she might have found someone to paint her?" Smith said.

Patti spooned some coffee into three cups. "I've only got instant if that's alright."

"Perfect," Smith said.

"I told her she had a face any artist would kill to paint. Oh my God..."

She teetered to the side, and Smith got up and helped her to one of the chairs.

"It's OK," he said. "I'll finish making the coffee."

"How could I say such a thing?" Patti rubbed her eyes and looked right at DC King. "What a horrible thing to say. I just meant that her features were perfect for art. She was so photogenic. Hold on..."

"What is it?" Smith said.

"Are you telling me she invited him in? Are you suggesting the man who did that to her – that *monster* was invited into my house?"

"We don't know that yet," DC King said. "Can you try to think hard. Are you sure Jennifer never mentioned anything about having her portrait painted?"

"She never spoke to me about it."

Smith brought the coffee to the table. "I couldn't find any sugar."

"I'll fetch it," Patti said.

"We believe Jennifer may have seen an advert somewhere," Smith said. "For someone who paints portraits. We don't know where she saw it, or what form the ad took. It could have been an advert in a shop window, or it might have been a flyer. Have you found anything like that lying around?"

"No," Patti said. "I would have noticed it."

"It's possible Jennifer kept it," DC King said. "She may have put it in her pocket."

"Would you mind having a quick look?" Smith asked. "The forensics officers have invaded your privacy enough – I don't want to go rifling through Jennifer's clothes. Finish your coffee first."

"What makes you so sure Jennifer got in touch with a portrait painter?" Patti said.

"We found some correspondence on her phone," DC King said.

"The messages were deleted," Smith added. "But we were able to retrieve them."

Patti started to laugh. It made Smith feel rather uncomfortable given the reason they were there.

"I'm sorry," she said. "You said the messages were deleted. I've known Jennifer for more than six years and I don't think she's ever deleted a single message in that time. I kept telling her that was why her phone was so slow sometimes. I went through it once with her, and there were WhatsApps from before we even met on her phone."

"She wasn't in the habit of clearing out her old stuff then?" DC King said.

"No."

Smith now knew he was correct in his assumption that *The Painter* was the one who deleted those messages.

"Where do you need me to look?" Patti said and stood up.

"Any coats or jackets Jennifer might have worn recently," Smith said.

"And perhaps the pockets of her jeans," DC King said.

"There's a full basket ready to be washed," Patti said. "I'll go and have a look."

She wasn't gone long.

"Nothing. I checked everything I could think of."

"It was a long shot," Smith said. "If it does turn up, could you give me a call."

He took out one of his cards and handed it to her.

She didn't take it. "I've already got one of those."

"DS Whitton gave her one," DC King explained. "She didn't have any of her own, but she thought one of yours was fine."

"No worries," Smith said.

Patti gave him a puzzled look.

"DS Whitton is my wife," he explained.

"That must make for an interesting life," Patti said.

"You're not wrong there," Smith said. "We won't keep you any longer."

CHAPTER TWENTY EIGHT

"Do I really have to watch this?"
Lionel Grange nodded to the screen of the laptop in front of him.
"No," Bridge told him. "You don't, but it would help us a lot if you could try and see if you remember anything else about Friday morning."

DC Moore started the footage.
"This might be upsetting for you," Bridge warned. "But I want you to look carefully at the person who gets out of the van in a minute."
Lionel watched the screen. The slow-walking old lady appeared to the left.
"That's Mrs Baker from number four," he said. "She makes a trip to the shops the same time every day. It's a five-minute walk – there and back, but it often takes her over an hour."

"The man is going to get out of the van now," DC Moore said.
The footage continued and DC Moore paused it when the driver of the van was halfway up the path.
"Do you recognise him?" Bridge said.
"How am I supposed to answer that?" Lionel said. "He's got his back to the camera."
"What about his height and build?" DC Moore said. "Do you know anyone who matches that description?"
"I don't think so. Don't you have any footage of his face?"
"I'm afraid not," Bridge said. "We believe he knew about the camera and made sure his face wasn't visible."

DC Moore resumed the footage. Lionel watched as the figure on the screen approached the front door. The door opened, whoever was behind it was forced back and Lionel gasped.
"I can't do this."
"It's alright," Bridge said. He nodded to DC Moore.

The footage was stopped, and the screen went blank.

"I'm sorry," Lionel said. "I can't do it."

"You don't have to watch any more of it," Bridge said.

"I could have stopped it, couldn't I?" Lionel said.

"It's not your fault," Bridge told him.

"No. If I hadn't booked that stupid holiday, Davina would still be alive."

"You can't blame yourself, Mr Grange," DC Moore said.

"Yes I can," Lionel said. "And I will blame myself for as long as I live. If I'd come straight home my fiancé would still be alive."

* * *

Kate Dawkins was the first of the eyewitnesses to arrive at the station. DI Smyth had been called into another meeting so Whitton spoke to her alone. She decided to keep it informal and took her up to the canteen.

"Would you like something to drink?" she asked. "We have a really good coffee machine."

"No thanks," Kate said.

Whitton guessed her age to be around the mid-twenties mark. She was a serious-looking woman with thick glasses.

"Can you tell me why you called the hotline?" Whitton said.

"Because I know the woman you're looking for. Her name is Paula Burton and we were in the same year at university."

"When was this?"

"About five or six years ago. We were studying History. Paula dropped out after the second year for financial reasons."

"And you're absolutely sure the woman we're looking for his her?"

"Positive," Kate said. "She's a very unusual looking woman. Not in a bad way, but she has a really memorable face."

"What do you do?" Whitton said. "Do you work in the city?"

"I stayed on at the university after I graduated. I did my Masters, and I'm in the middle of my PhD. I do the odd lecture, and I'm hoping to get a full-time position soon. Why are you looking for Paula? What has she done?"

"We just need to find her," Whitton said. "You said you saw her yesterday. Where was this?"

"Just past the pizza shop on Hull Road. I spotted her and we had a bit of a chat."

"What time was this?"

"Around lunchtime," Kate said. "It was – I'd just come from the hairdresser. It was about half-twelve."

"What did you talk about?"

"Not much. Small talk. She seemed very keen to get away to be honest. She said she had an appointment."

"What kind of appointment?"

"With a friend. She said her friend was an art student and she wanted to paint Paula to put in her portfolio. I suppose Paula does have an interesting face, and I imagine she'd make a good subject."

"Did Paula mention a name?" Whitton said.

"No. She just said she had to go because her friend was going to paint her portrait."

"Were you and Paula friends during your time together at university?" Whitton said.

"I wouldn't go that far," Kate said. "We were in the same classes, but we hardly socialised."

"Can you remember the people she did hang around with?"

"I wasn't really into going out much. I love history, and that's all I focused on. Why are you really so keen to find Paula? The appeal was rather vague."

"I'm afraid I can't go into that. Can you remember anything else about yesterday? Did Paula seem anxious at all?"

"I suppose she was," Kate said. "She was in quite a hurry to get away from me. She said she really needed to keep the appointment with her friend. When you think about it, it seems a bit strange, doesn't it?"

"What do you mean?" Whitton said.

"If it's a friend, why stress so much about getting there on time? Surely if she was going to see a friend that friend wouldn't really mind if she was a few minutes late."

CHAPTER TWENTY NINE

It was the second eyewitness who provided them with the break they were looking for. Gordon Parks remembered seeing a woman matching the description of the one in the public appeal. He was walking his dog in Heslington and the Yorkie managed to slip out of its collar. It ran off and when Gordon was chasing it he caught a glimpse of a woman outside one of the houses in Norman Street. That brief glance was enough. The woman had a very memorable face, and Gordon was convinced it was the same woman as the one he'd seen on the news.

Gordon couldn't recall the exact house she was standing outside but he was able to narrow it down to four terraced properties in the middle of the row, and after checking the first three, the uniforms who were dispatched made the gruesome discovery inside number 26. A woman was lying on her back on the floor in the living room. The carpet her head was resting on was drenched in blood and she had a deep laceration in her neck. On her chest was a painting of her while she was clearly still alive and well. PC Simon Miller would dream about the big brown eyes in the portrait for a very long time afterwards.

Smith didn't attend. He'd expected her to be found and he wasn't interested in taking a look at the crime scene. He was more focused on the painting that he knew would be somewhere near the body. He asked Billie Jones to take as many photographs as she could and he asked her to forward them to him as soon as possible.

The driving license in the dead woman's pocket confirmed that she was Paula Burton. Kate Dawkins had been right. Whitton and DI Smyth had come straight to Norman Street when the call had come in and they were now standing outside number 26.

"Kate Dawkins mentioned something about Paula meeting a friend," Whitton told DI Smyth. "She said she was going to paint Paula's portrait for her portfolio."

"Bridge and DC Moore have gone to break the news to the parents," DI Smyth said. "Could you get hold of them and tell them to ask about this friend?"

Whitton sent Bridge a short message and he replied shortly afterwards with a thumbs up.

"Do we know who lives here?" Whitton asked.

"According to the woman who lives next door," DI Smyth said. "The place has been vacant since the end of the university term. She couldn't tell us who the landlord is, but it'll be easy to find out. Where is that husband of yours? I've never known Smith not to come to the scene of a murder."

"He's more interested in the painting," Whitton said. "He's determined to find a clue about the next victim. This case is starting to consume him?"

"What's new?"

"No, this one's different. He's taking it more personally than he usually does. I think it's because the killer is in contact with him, and he feels responsible for the women's deaths. Have you seen the painting?"

"Not yet," DI Smyth said. "Billie and Pete are still busy in there, and I don't want to get in their way."

"Is Webber not here?"

DI Smyth shook his head. "What's the full story there?"

"The DI you replaced was killed in very similar circumstances. She and Webber were planning to get married, and this is bound to bring some terrible memories back to the surface."

"This job is enough to send a person to a madhouse," DI Smyth said.

A black Toyota pulled up - Bridge and DC Moore got out and walked over to Whitton and DI Smyth.

"Paula Burton's parents couldn't think of any friends of hers who are art students," Bridge said.

"When was the last time they saw her?" Whitton asked.

"Not since last week," DC Moore said. "She has her own flat apparently."

"Do we know if she lives alone?" DI Smyth said.

"She does," Bridge confirmed.

"We asked her mother if she'd heard Paula talking about getting her portrait painted," DC Moore said. "And that's when she broke down. We couldn't get anything else out of her, and the father wasn't bearing up much better."

"OK," DI Smyth said. "I think the best way to proceed is this: we'll split into two teams. One team will go through the motions and speak to friends and family members of the victim. The other will focus on the painting and only the painting. If *The Painter* follows the same pattern as in the other murders, it's likely there's a clue to his next victim in the painting inside that house. I'll give Smith a call and see what his thoughts are on this."

He took out his phone and walked away.

"I'm happy to be on either team," Bridge said.

"Me too," DC Moore seconded.

"Has Webber finished with the painting?" Bridge asked.

"He's not here," Whitton told him.

"The poor bastard."

DI Smyth came back over. "Billie Jones has forwarded some photos of the painting to Smith. He and DC King are already making a start on it. I suggested that PC Griffin lend a hand."

"Smith must have loved that," Bridge said.

"He wasn't particularly fazed to be honest. Baldwin is also on board with it, so we'll deal with the victim. How was she picked, and how did *The Painter* manage to get her to come here?"

"Perhaps she saw the same advert as Jennifer Cole," DC Moore said.

"It's very possible," DI Smyth said. "But where did they see it? We need to look for a link between the two women. Where have they crossed paths and whereabouts on those paths did they see the advert offering portrait painting? Before we look into that, I want a thorough door-to-door underway. There are plenty of uniforms on the scene."

"I'll get onto it," DC Moore offered.

"Thanks, Harry."

Billie Jones came out of number 26 and stretched her arms. She removed her protective gloves and put them inside a plastic bag. She walked over to the three detectives.

"Are you OK?" Bridge asked her.

"Not really," Billie said. "I know her."

CHAPTER THIRTY

The latest of *The Painter's* pieces of art was different to the others in that there was no background. The painting of Paula Burton was a traditional portrait with Paula looking directly at the artist. Smith wondered where a possible clue could be lurking in a piece that was not much more than a portrayal of a woman's face.

Paula Burton was indeed a striking looking young woman. Her large brown eyes, button nose and high forehead lent her a noble look. Her face was framed with thick, curly black hair. There were no signs of injury on her face, and Smith deduced she'd been painted before she was killed.

"This is going to be a tricky one," DC King said.

She was sitting next to him in the small conference room. Baldwin was on the other side. Smith had suggested to PC Griffin that he find somewhere quiet to scrutinise the photographs for the sole reason that he couldn't stand to be anywhere near the man. They might have been forced to work together but DI Smyth didn't specify that it had to be in the same room.

"I know," Smith said. "How can there possibly be a clue about the next victim in another woman's face?"

"Was there anything else in the painting itself?" Baldwin said. "The original, I mean."

"Billie took photographs from all angles," Smith told her. "What we're looking at now is what we'd see if we were looking at the one *The Painter* painted."

"I really don't know what he could hide in a woman's face," DC King said.

"Do we have a photo of Paula?" Baldwin said. "Perhaps he's altered her appearance somehow."

Smith clicked the bottom of the screen and a photograph appeared. He positioned it so it was side by side with the portrait.

"I can't see any obvious differences," Smith said. "He's managed to capture her very well. He's even got the tiny mole on her cheek spot on."

"Do you think it's possible we can't see any clues about the next victim because there isn't one?" It was Baldwin.

"Are you suggesting he could be finished?" Smith said.

"It's possible," DC King said.

"No, I don't think he would have bothered to paint her if that was the case. There is something here and we just haven't spotted it yet."

"She's wearing a pendant," Baldwin said. "Can we zoom in on that?"

Smith did, and all he could see was a small gold charm on a gold chain."

"It looks like one of those dreamcatchers," DC King said.

"It didn't work for Paula, did it?" Smith mused. "Her dreams were definitely not realised."

He looked up when PC Griffin came into the room.

"I think I might have found something," the beak-nosed PC said.

"Could you do me a favour?" Smith said.

"What?"

"At least do me the courtesy of addressing me as, Sarge – everybody else does every once in a while. Can you do that?"

"Of course, Sarge."

"What have you found?" DC King asked. "Have you found something in the painting?"

"I figured that three pairs of eyes were sufficient," PC Griffin said.

Smith glared at him. "You decided to make that call on your own, did you?"

"I might have found a link between the victims, Sarge."

"I'm listening."

PC Griffin placed some sheets of paper on the table in front of Smith.

"This is a Facebook group that was taken down a few years ago."

Smith looked at the paper. It was a printout of a home screen of something called *Art4Fun*.

"You said it was taken down?" he said. "How did you manage to get hold of it?"

"Even obsolete social media is still accessible," PC Griffin said. "The group no longer exists but archived posts are still there to view."

"What is this *Art4Fun*?" DC King said.

"It appears to be a forum for amateur artists to post their work," PC Griffin said. "And Jennifer Cole, Davina Hawkins and Paula Burton were all members."

Smith looked at him, and he realised that if he wasn't such an obnoxious human being he might be tempted to pat him on the back.

"What prompted you to even consider looking for this?" he asked instead.

"It's 2021, Sarge," PC Griffin said. "Social media is an exceptionally useful tool in modern day detection."

"This could be the link we've been looking for," Smith said. "What else do we know about this group?"

"Like I said, it was deleted a few years ago. At the end of 2018 to be exact, but what are the odds on three of the victims of *The Painter* being on the same Facebook group?"

"Do we know anything about the group admin?" Baldwin said. "Or the other members of the group?"

"We're going to have to dig deeper," PC Griffin said. "The members list isn't there anymore, and getting any info from Facebook itself can be very time-consuming. We're talking court orders and the like."

"We don't have that kind of time to waste," Smith said. "If the members list isn't there, how did you find the link between the victims?"

"Lucky break, Sarge. All three of them happened to post their work on the page before it was taken down."

"Did anyone else do the same?" Baldwin said.

"A few people," PC Griffin said. "But none of them have come up in the course of the investigation as far as I'm aware. I've made a list."

This was on the second sheet of paper. There were only seven names on it, but Smith instantly recognised two of them. The third name on the list was someone they'd spoken to very recently. It was Henry Harvey. The co-owner of Harvey's Couriers had belonged to the same Facebook group of three of the victims of *The Painter*.

The name at the bottom of the list was infinitely more concerning for Smith and he found his eyes glued to the name of the woman at the bottom of the page. He knew her well. He should do – he'd lived next door to the woman for a few years now, and his daughter was best friends with her daughter. The last name on the list was Sheila Rogers.

CHAPTER THIRTY ONE

"It was just a bit of fun."

Shelia Rogers had been surprised to see Smith and DC King on her doorstep. Smith had stood there many times before, but this was the first occasion where his presence there was for police business. Smith had explained the nature of their visit, and Sheila had invited them in. Fortunately, Sheila's daughter Fran was next door with Laura. Smith was glad – he didn't want to cause the young girls any distress.

Sheila sat down opposite Smith and DC King in the living room.

"The names of two of the victims have been published in the press," Smith said.

Paula Burton's identity hadn't yet been released.

"Didn't you recognise their names?" he added.

"I very rarely watch the news," Sheila said.

"Three women have been killed," DC King said. "And all of them were members of the *Art4Fun* Facebook group."

"Did you ever post anything on the group?" Smith asked.

"Once or twice," Sheila said.

"I didn't even know you were an artist."

"I wouldn't call myself an artist, but I do like to paint. What happened to these women?"

It was all over the news and social media so Smith decided to tell her everything.

"Three women were murdered by someone who calls himself *The Painter*," he said. "I can't go into too much detail but there were distinct similarities between the murder scenes. And now we know that all three victims were members of an old Facebook group. What else can you tell us about this group? Do you know who set it up?"

"It was quite a while ago," Sheila said. "Can't you find out? You've got specialists for that kind of thing, haven't you?"

"Anything Facebook related takes an awful lot of time," DC King explained. "There is a lot of legal red tape to get past."

"I can't remember who started the group," Shelia said.

"How did you hear about it?" Smith said.

"I think it was recommended to me. You know how the Internet works – you buy something online and the next thing you know, you're inundated with similar stuff."

"Was this group exclusively online?" Smith said.

"I'm not following you," Sheila said.

"Did you ever meet any of the members in person?"

"Yes."

Smith could feel his face heating up. It was a sensation he'd experienced many times before, and it was a feeling he usually got when he was on the verge of unravelling an important piece of the fabric of an investigation.

"Go on," he said.

"I remember they advertised a workshop," Sheila said.

"Was it here in York?"

Sheila nodded.

"When?" Smith said. "Do you remember when it was? And where?"

"It was before I moved next door to you," Sheila said. "Before the divorce. I can't give you an exact time and place."

"We need you to think, Sheila," Smith said. "This is extremely important."

"I really can't remember."

"What about your ex-husband? Is it possible he will remember?"

"That idiot?" Sheila said. "I very much doubt it."

"Do you have his contact details?" DC King asked. "We can ask him about it."

"You don't have to get involved," Smith promised

"I don't have any contact whatsoever with that man," Sheila said. "All I know is he's somewhere in Canada and I wouldn't care if he never got in touch ever again. He didn't even make an effort to phone Fran on her birthday."

"I'm sorry about that," Smith said.

"What happened at the workshops?" DC King said.

"Not much," Sheila told her. "There were only a handful of us and we were all asked to talk about ourselves. I thought we'd at least get the chance to learn something, but it was more a social event where we drank wine and talked about our paintings."

"Who organised it?" Smith said.

"I can't remember. I'm sorry I can't be more helpful."

"Was that the only workshop the *Art4Fun* group organised?" DC King said.

"I think there were more," Sheila said. "But I didn't bother going to any of the others."

The front door opened and slammed, and Laura and Fran burst into the room. The expression on Laura's face was one of utter bewilderment. She really wasn't expecting to see her father there.

"We're just having a chat," Smith told her.

That was enough of an explanation for the young girl.

"Can we go to the park?" Fran asked Sheila. "Darren and Lucy are taking Andrew out, and we want to go too."

"If it's OK with them it's OK with me," Sheila said.

"Me too," Smith said.

Laura's gaze lingered on Smith's face for a moment then she followed her friend out of the room. He heard their steps as they thundered up the stairs, the front door slammed again, and everything was quiet.

"Do I need to be concerned?" Sheila asked.

"I don't know," Smith admitted.

"You say that three of the women in that group are dead. What if this painter is ticking them off from a list? What if my name is on that list?"

"I really don't know if you're in danger or not, Sheila."

"That makes me feel a whole lot better."

"But what we do know," Smith said. "Are a few things about how he operates. Have you had any uninvited visitors recently? Any strangers knocking on your door?"

"Not that I can remember."

"And you haven't had the feeling that you were being watched?" DC King said.

"No," Sheila said. "Nothing like that. You're scaring me now. Don't you have some kind of protective custody in cases like these?"

"Unfortunately not," Smith said. "We can't get authorisation for that without absolute proof that a person's life is in immediate danger. But I'll be next door, as will Erica, and if you hear so much as a bump in the night, I want you to call us. It doesn't matter what time it is. We have to go. I want you to lock the doors when we're gone. And keep your phone on you at all times."

"I'm scared, Jason," Sheila said on the doorstep.

"We're doing everything we can to find this man," Smith promised.

"What about Fran? What if he hurts Fran? I couldn't live with myself if anything happened to her."

"I will do everything I can to catch him. That's a promise."

"Can Fran stay with you tonight?"

"Of course," Smith said. "Lock the doors behind us."

CHAPTER THIRTY TWO

Taylor Jenkins had been told her dream of a shop offering all things new age was precisely that. It was a pipedream, and it would probably fold within six months. Friends and family alike had warned her that there was no market for so-called *Hippy* products anymore. The serious-looking man at the bank had echoed these sentiments. What she proposed simply wasn't viable in the current market. Consequently, her application for a business loan was rejected. The bank couldn't risk lending on the basis of what Taylor had proposed. Hopes and dreams did not equate to future profits.

Taylor hadn't given up. She didn't need the backing of her narrow-minded friends and family, and the rejection of the business loan only served to spur her on. She was going to prove the whole fucking lot of them wrong. She started small – a market stall on the weekend, and the odd festival here and there, and she managed to build enough of a following to return to the bank with a more promising proposal.

It still wasn't enough. Taylor's business model had no consistency to it. Even when she pointed out that the market for her specialised products was on an upward turn the man at the bank told her it still wasn't viable.

Taylor's lucky break came from an unexpected source. A painting an aunt had left her when she died turned out to be considerably more valuable than Taylor would have ever believed. She'd never particularly liked the piece and she had no hesitation in parting with it when she heard the price that was offered. Taylor now had enough to fork out for a years' rent on a small shop smack bang in the middle of the tourist hub of the city, with plenty left over to stock the shop to the hilt.

Six months later the shop had grown into one of the most popular outlets in the heart of York, and Taylor was able to stock even more. She sourced healing crystals from Australia – balms, oils and candles from the Middle

East, and herbs and bath salts from South America. She stocked a wide variety of homemade jewellery, and clothing from local producers, and her new Feng Sui range of products had literally flown off the shelves quicker than she could restock them.

Taylor's personal favourite had always been her dreamcatchers. She made these herself, and she'd become very good at it. An idea for a new design of dreamcatcher had come to her in the early hours of the morning, and she was keen to get started on making the concept a reality. It was lunchtime, and she'd been glad when her assistant had turned the sign on the entrance round so it now read *Closed for lunch*.

The templates were laid out on the table in the storeroom of the shop, ready to be turned into something unique and beautiful. Taylor took a bite of her sandwich and closed her eyes. Her idea involved spiders. The Ojibwe Indians of the Great Lakes considered the spider to be a symbol of protection and hope, and Taylor wanted to create something based on the legend of the old lady, Nokomis. The elderly grandmother, upon seeing her grandson about to kill a spider, stops him. The spider, grateful for her saving his life rewards her by spinning a magic web around her to ward off evil.

Taylor finished her sandwich and turned her attention to the dreamcatcher. She made a start on the black web in the centre of the circle. She was putting the finishing touches to the outer stitching when a noise from the shop stopped her dead.

"Hello," the voice was heard again.

It was a familiar voice. Taylor definitely recognised it.

"We're closed for lunch," she called back.

Then something occurred to her. Vanya, her assistant was supposed to have locked the door when she turned the sign round. Clearly, she hadn't. Taylor put the dreamcatcher down and went to see who it was.

The unwelcome customer was taking a keen interest in the Feng Sui display next to the counter.

"This is all wrong."

"I created that display according to principles set out centuries ago," Taylor argued.

"You cannot have metal and wood objects positioned like this. The positive energy inside this shop has no channel to pass through. Surely you can feel it."

The customer remained standing with her back to Taylor.

"Feel what?" Taylor said. "Do I know you?"

"There is bad energy here."

"Who are you?" Taylor asked. "I recognise your voice."

The self-proclaimed Feng Sui expert turned around, and Taylor gasped. "You?"

They held eye contact for quite some time, and Taylor found herself unable to look away. That's why she didn't see the flash of the blade until it was directly below her field of vision. Her throat was sliced open so quickly, she didn't have time to gasp a last lungful of air. Another slash came from the opposite side. Taylor remained on her feet for a few seconds, her eyes fell back in their sockets, and she collapsed onto the display of healing crystals. None of them were going to help her now.

The Painter got to work. There wasn't much time. The multicoloured crystals would make an interesting background. After taking a number of photographs from different angles it was time to leave. It wasn't possible to complete the painting here – it would be done later and then an email would be sent to Detective Jason Smith.

Unbeknown to *The Painter*, there was a silent observer keeping an eye on the proceedings. The unblinking eye of the hidden camera inside the mouth of one of the African masks was taking it all in. The camera had been set up after Taylor Jenkins suspected her assistant of helping herself to the stock. Unfortunately, it was highly unlikely the footage from the camera would ever see the light of day. The only person who was aware of it was no longer alive.

CHAPTER THIRTY THREE

"Henry Harvey has disappeared off the radar," Smith told DI Smyth inside his office.
After considering what PC Griffin had turned up about the Facebook group the co-owner of the courier company was once again a definite person of interest.

"He's not at work," Smith said. "And he's not at home."
"Are you sure about this?" DI Smyth said.
"Why didn't he mention the fact that he knew two of the victims, boss?"
"Perhaps he hasn't been watching the news."
"I'm not talking about the news," Smith said. "I asked him if he knew Jennifer Price and Davina Hawkins and he denied it. He was a member of that Facebook group and when I asked him if he paints, he said he did. He had access to that van, and he cannot provide an alibi for the times of the first two murders."
"We'll find him," DI Smyth said. "And we'll bring him in for questioning. What was your initial impression of him?"
"He's a charmer. Good looking bloke, and I reckon he's always been a big hit with the ladies. I got the feeling he's well practiced in the art of seduction. We need to search his house."
"I'm not going to play this game with you again, Smith."
"I'm not talking about going the warrant route."
"What other route is there?" DI Smyth said.
"I ask him nicely. Explain to him that if he's got nothing to hide, he's got nothing to worry about."
"Do you really believe he's *The Painter*?" DI Smyth said.
"I didn't get the impression that he was a cold-blooded killer, boss, but it's been a while and I reckon I've got a bit rusty. We've got enough pointing in

his direction to justify arresting him."

"I'll put the word out. Have you had any luck with the painting of Paula Burton?"

"There's nothing in the painting but her face," Smith said. "I can't see where a clue to the next victim could be hidden."

"Have you considered the possibility that's because there will be no next victim?"

"For precisely two seconds. Why bother painting her if he's not going to give us another clue?"

"Have you received anymore emails from him?"

"Not a sausage," Smith said. "But that means nothing. Perhaps he's delaying for a reason. Perhaps he's already taken his next victim. All I know is three of us examined that painting and neither me, Kerry or Baldwin could find anything."

"What was PC Griffin doing?" DI Smyth said. "He was supposed to be assisting you."

"Griffin was the one who came up with the link between the victims, boss."

"I see."

"And as much as I hate to admit it, the man has been an asset to the team so far. He seems to have a knack for knowing exactly where to look."

"Does that mean you're slowly becoming a fan of his?"

"I wouldn't go that far," Smith said. "He got the GPS coordinates straight away, and now he's come up with the first link. He's either very sharp, or he's involved in the murders, and I very much doubt the moron has it in him to kill."

"Stranger things have happened. What's the next item on the agenda?"

"I want to ask a favour."

"Is this going to come back to bite me on the backside?" DI Smyth said.

"I don't think so. My next-door-neighbour was also in that Facebook group. She attended one of the workshops they held in the city, and she's terrified. We don't have enough to justify protection, but I'm sure we can stretch to a bit of extra police presence outside her house."

"I'll arrange for some uniforms to do a few extra patrols in the area," DI Smyth said.

"I appreciate it," Smith told him. "I think she'll be safe. I asked her about any suspicious callers, and she told me she hasn't noticed anyone strange hanging around, but I promised her I'd keep an eye out for her."

"What about the other names on the list?" DI Smyth said. "What do we know about them?"

"There were only seven we could find from the archived Facebook posts," Smith said. "Three are already dead, one is missing in action, and a fifth lives next door to me. We've managed to track down one of the remaining two – Taylor Jenkins. She owns some kind of hippy shop not far from The Shambles, and I've asked Harry and Kerry to go and have a chat to her there. The last one is a woman by the name of Gaynor Lovelace and she's dead. She was killed in a car crash a couple of years ago."

"I find it hard to believe there were only seven members in that group."

"There were probably more," Smith agreed. "But it'll be tricky to find them. You know what it's like with Facebook – it's a rule unto itself where the law is concerned. Getting anything out of them takes time, and time is something we don't have the luxury of. This killer works extremely quickly."

"Do you think there's any point in an afternoon briefing?"

"No," Smith said. "Not until we have something concrete to discuss."

"I thought so."

"I wondered if we should broadcast another public appeal."

"What kind of appeal?"

"Asking anyone who was on the *Art4Fun* Facebook group to come forward," Smith explained.

"No," DI Smyth said without thinking.

"It might give us a better idea of who else was in that group."

"And it will scare the living daylights out of the past members in the process."

"I wasn't suggesting we tell them the reason we're looking for them."

"The answer is no," DI Smyth said.

The tone of his voice told Smith this was not up for debate.

"I'd better get back to work," he said. "Let me know the moment Henry Harvey shows up."

He left the office and made his way outside for a cigarette. He bumped into Bridge on the way out.

"Billie knows the third victim," Bridge said.

"I'm going out for a smoke," Smith said. "We can talk outside."

Bridge came out with him.

Smith lit a cigarette. "How does Billie know Paula Burton?"

"They went to school together," Bridge said.

"Were they friends?"

"Apparently so. They drifted apart when they left school – Billie went to university in Leeds, and Paula remained in York, but they were quite close at school."

"What can Billie tell us about her?" Smith said.

"She was a bit of a loner at school. She didn't have many friends and apparently, she was the butt of a lot of cruel bullying."

"But she and Billie became friends?"

"Billie has always found herself drawn to the outcasts," Bridge said. "The oddballs of society."

"Yourself excluded of course."

"Naturally," Bridge said.

"Is she alright?" Smith asked.

"I think it was more of a shock than anything else. You don't expect to go to work and come across the corpse of someone you went to school with. She hadn't seen Paula for years."

Smith's phone beeped in his pocket. It was an unfamiliar tone, and when he swiped the screen, he realised why that was. He'd turned on the notification tone for his Gmail and he'd received an email.

"Fuck," he said after reading the first line.

"What is it?" Bridge said.

Smith read the entire email out loud.

"Time has run out, Detective Australia. Perhaps you'll up your game with the next one. I sincerely hope so. I'll be in touch soon. *The Painter.*"

"What did he mean by that?" Bridge said.

"What the fuck do you think he meant? Somewhere out there is another dead woman with a painting next to her. He's playing with us. How were we supposed to get anything from a portrait of a woman? There was nothing in that painting apart from the woman's face."

The phone sounded again but this time it was an incoming call. The name on the screen was DC King's.

"Kerry," Smith answered it.

"Taylor Jenkins is dead, Sarge."

Even though Smith had been expecting it, it still felt like someone had scooped out everything inside him and cast it aside. He felt utterly empty.

"Are you still there?" DC King said.

"I'm still here."

"There's no painting."

"What?" Smith said.

"Taylor Jenkins was on that list, her throat has been sliced open, but we couldn't find a painting anywhere."

CHAPTER THIRTY FOUR

It took Smith quite a while to get through the crowd of people gathered behind the police tape that had been erected around the shops. From a cordoning off perspective, Energy Emporium was a nightmare. Located smack bang in the middle of the row of shops on a narrow strip of pavement, it had been a time-consuming process. The DCs King and Moore had needed to speak to the people working in the adjacent shops to make sure they didn't let any more customers inside. It was late July – the tourist season was in full swing, and none of the shopkeepers were happy about it.

Smith finally managed to squeeze through the horde of people and ducked underneath the tape. PC Simon Miller was standing on the other side, preventing members of the public from going any further.
"You need to widen the cordon," Smith told him. "The rubberneckers are too close."
"How far back do you need it to go, Sarge," PC Miller asked.
"As far as the end of the arcade. Have the people in the nearby shops been told to remain where they are?"
"They have, Sarge. DC King made sure of it."
Smith knew she would. It's possible someone in one of the adjacent businesses saw the person who went inside Energy Emporium.

Smith had come prepared. He eased himself into the SOC suit and looked at his reflection in the window of the shop. Grant Webber had been correct – the suit was definitely too tight and Smith was shocked by the bulge in his stomach. He sucked in his belly and decided it was a trick of the light. The reflection in the glass was distorted somehow.

The first thing Smith realised when he went inside the shop was that Grant Webber was present. The Head of Forensics had turned up this time. He was barking orders to Pete Richards somewhere at the back of the shop.

Smith couldn't make out everything that was said but one of the words was quite clear – *dreamcatcher*.

Smith walked towards the back of the shop. He stopped to look at some of the things for sale, but he didn't actually know what most of them were supposed to be. There was a shelf of what appeared to be some kind of rock. Coloured stones of all shapes and sizes were lined up in no particular order. Another shelf contained bottles of mystery lotions and potions. Smith wondered what kind of people bought this stuff. He cast a glance at the dead woman on the floor and carried on towards the back of the shop.

He found Webber and Pete in the storeroom. Unopened boxes were stacked on the floor in the corner. A table against one of the walls was covered with hoops of some sort.

"That suit is far too small for you," Webber said.

"So you keep saying," Smith said. "Glad you could make it."

"It's my job."

"What are they?" Smith pointed to the hoops on the table.

"Dreamcatchers," Pete Richards said. "Or at least they would have been if she'd been allowed to finish them. According to the other woman who works here, Taylor Jenkins was making quite a name for herself with these things."

Smith looked closely at the unfinished dreamcatchers. One of them was almost complete. A spider web had been stitched inside the centre of the hoop, and two black spiders hung from opposite sides of the circle.

"One of these things was in the painting of Paula Burton, wasn't it?"

"The third victim," Pete said for the benefit of Webber.

"She was wearing a pendant shaped like a dreamcatcher around her neck," the Head of Forensics said.

"And I missed its significance," Smith said.

"Don't beat yourself up about it," Webber said. "It was the vaguest of clues at best, and there's no way you could have linked it to the poor woman in there."

He nodded to the door that separated the shop from the storeroom."

"Why bother with the pendant when he knew it would take a miracle to tie it to Taylor Jenkins?" Smith wondered out loud.

"I believe you need to stop working on the assumption that *The Painter's* intentions are altruistic," Webber said. "The most advanced codebreakers in the world wouldn't be able to crack these ones in the time he's allowed. It just isn't possible."

"Why is he doing it?" Smith said.

"Motive is your department," Webber reminded him.

"You're dead right there. It's good to have you back."

Smith went back inside the shop. He waited for Billie to finish taking photographs of the positioning of the body and crouched down to get a better look. Taylor Jenkins had died from what appeared to be a single laceration to her neck. The wound was deep, and Smith knew it would be impossible to survive such an injury. The amount of blood on and around the body suggested the carotid arteries had been severed.

"She was standing up when he did this to her," Billie said. "The arterial spurt is the second longest I've ever seen."

"Are you telling me you measured it?" Smith said.

"Of course. She was on her feet when the fatal incision was made, and I believe she was face to face with her killer when it happened."

Smith nodded. "Go on."

He wasn't expecting what happened next. Before he knew what was happening Billie was behind him with her arm around his neck.

"Bridge never warned me about this side of you," Smith said.

"Rupert has yet to experience this side of me," she said. "Keep still. You slit someone's throat from behind, you press the knife down hard and slice in one quick motion."

She demonstrated this with her index finger.

"You need to cut your nails," Smith said.

Billie made no comment on this.

"However," she continued. "If you look at the lacerations in her neck you'll see two distinct wounds. Dr Bean will confirm that the victim had her neck slashed open from two opposite directions. Her killer was standing a few feet in front of her."

"What does that tell us?" Smith said.

"You tell me."

"She knew him, didn't she?"

Billie's reply consisted of a smile.

"She did," Smith said. "She was acquainted with the bastard who did this to her."

CHAPTER THIRTY FIVE

"Taylor Jenkins had no defensive wounds because she knew her killer." Smith knew this was significant. DI Smyth wasn't planning on holding an afternoon briefing but in light of what had happened at Energy Emporium that had changed. He'd informed Smith that he was running late and he told Smith to make a start without him.

"She was standing facing him when he struck," Smith explained further. "Billie mentioned something about an arterial spurt. She measured the distance of it and she said it was the second longest she'd ever seen."

"If she was standing facing him," DC King said. "It would be impossible for him not to get some of her blood on his clothes."

"That's right. But unless we happen to find those clothes, it doesn't help us. I want to focus on the way she was killed. She didn't react to the attack because she wasn't expecting it. It was the last thing on her mind."

"She didn't feel threatened by him," DC King said.

"She must have read about the other murders," Bridge pointed out. "The news has consisted of very little else over the past few days. And she must have made the connection with the art group, so why wasn't she on guard?"

"That's a very good question," Smith said. "And as far as I can see there are only two possible answers to it."

If Smith was waiting for someone to guess what they could be, he was about to be disappointed. The silence inside the small conference room told him he was on his own with this one.

"Either she hadn't figured out the link between the victims and the *Art4Fun* Facebook group," he said. "Or she had spotted the connection, but the person who killed her wasn't someone she associated with that group."

"What exactly are you saying?" DC Moore said. "That the link is the group, but the killer is someone who wasn't a member of that group? That's completely nonsensical even by your standards."

"All of the victims have been women who were members of the art group," DC King said. "And I think that's what DS Smith is saying. They were *victims*. They were selected because of something to do with the Facebook group but it doesn't necessarily mean the killer was also a member. In fact, it's more likely that he wasn't."

"But we've just established that Taylor knew him," DC Moore remined them.

"Perhaps he was someone in the periphery of the group," Whitton suggested. "What else do we know about that group?"

"I think the actual Facebook part isn't worth focusing on," Smith said. "It's a virtual environment, and even though things have been known to have turned ugly on social media it doesn't exist beyond the realms of the Internet."

"The workshops," DC King said. "Something happened at those workshops, didn't it?"

"It's the only explanation," Smith said. "Sheila Rogers told us she only attended the first one. Not much was achieved so she didn't go to any of the others. That's what we need to focus on. So far we've been concentrating on the where, when, and how, and I think it's high time we took a look at the most important aspect."

"Motive." Whitton did the honours.

"What took you so long?" DC Moore dared.

"I'm out of practice," Smith said. "But now I'm back. Why did this killer target these women? What does he get out of it?"

"All four murders strike me as killing out of hatred," DC King said. "There was a lot of violence at play in all of them."

"No," Smith disagreed. "The first two victims were drugged first. There was a certain amount of compassion on display there."

"What other motives are there?" DC Moore said. "Financial gain. That one doesn't apply here. Love? I don't think so."

"Revenge is always a good one," Bridge said.

"And it's the one I'm leaning towards in this instance," Smith said. "I'm not quite sure why, but..."

"You'll let us know when you've figured it out?" Whitton guessed.

"Something like that."

"Can we assume that he's finished?" DC Moore asked.

"Why would we do that?" Smith said.

"There was no painting. He didn't paint her and there was no clue about the next victim. The logical assumption to make out of that is there will be no next victim."

"We can't afford to think like that."

"Why not? In my book, no painting equates to no more victims. He's finished what he's set out to do, and it's possible he's long gone. He could be halfway across the Channel by now, never to be seen again."

"I want you to keep an open mind about a possible motive," Smith said. "Think hard about it and don't stop thinking about it. I want to discuss possible suspects. From past experience, it is almost always someone we've crossed paths with somewhere during the course of the investigation. Any thoughts?"

"Henry Harvey is the most obvious one, Sarge," DC Moore said.

"He is. He has no alibi for any of the murders, he had access to the vehicle that was used in two of them, and he was a member of that *Art4Fun* Facebook group. Add to that the fact that he's conveniently disappeared, I'd say he's top of the list. Anybody else?"

"Sheila Rogers?" Bridge said.

"What?" Smith and Whitton said in unison.

Bridge held up his hands. "I'm just going on what the facts tell us. Sheila is the only person on that list besides Henry Harvey who is still alive. What do we know about her?"

"She's a primary school teaching assistant," Whitton said. "Her daughter happens to be our daughter's best friend."

"Does she have your personal email address?" Bridge said. "*The Painter* has been corresponding with you on that email address."

"Sheila Rogers is not a serial killer," Smith insisted.

"I appreciate that she's a friend of yours," Bridge said. "But in case you've forgotten, friends of yours have surprised you in the past."

"I think I would know if the mother of my daughter's best mate was a psychopath, Bridge. Any other suggestions?"

"Henry Harvey is my odds-on favourite," DC King said.

"Mine too," DC Moore said.

"I agree." It was Whitton

"I'm glad we're all on the same page about something," Smith said. "Now all we need to do is find the man."

CHAPTER THIRTY SIX

By four that afternoon Henry Harvey still hadn't been found. His brother, John had promised to get in touch if he did hear from him, but so far, the man who was now the main suspect in *The Painter* investigation had proved to be elusive. Smith had decided that the best way to proceed in Henry's absence was to revisit the victims and look at them more closely, taking what they knew about the *Art4Fun* group into consideration.

Energy Emporium was closed for the foreseeable future, and Vanya Green, Taylor Jenkins' assistant was surplus to requirements. Bridge and DC Moore were now sitting opposite her in her apartment in Rowntree Park. Vanya was a short, squat woman with nervous eyes. Bridge noticed they never stopped moving behind her pink glasses.

"How are you feeling?" DC Moore asked her.
"Numb," Vanya said. "I still can't believe it. It doesn't feel real."
"Where are you from?" DC Moore said. "I know that accent."
"Hendon," Vanya said. "I've been in York for five years now. You?"
"Nowhere near as posh as Hendon," the man from London said. "Wimbledon. What made you move up north?"
"I had my reasons."
DC Moore didn't press any further.
"How long have you been working at Energy Emporium?" Bridge said.
"Since the beginning," Vanya said. "2018."
"So you knew Taylor well then?"
"I suppose so. She was alright, although she could be a bit narky sometimes."
"She had a temper on her?" DC Moore said.
"I don't want to speak ill of the dead. I mean, she's barely cold, isn't she?"
"Go on," Bridge said.

"She didn't trust anyone," Vanya said. "She was always watching the customers like a hawk in case they tried to nick something."

"It happens," DC Moore said.

"She didn't have cameras inside the shop, did she?" Bridge said.

"Oddly not," Vanya said. "I don't know why."

"Do you know much about her family and friends?" Bridge asked.

"We didn't really socialise out of work," Vanya said.

"She wasn't married, was she?" DC Moore said.

Vanya shook her head.

"What about a boyfriend?" Bridge said. "Did she ever mention anything about a boyfriend."

Vanya started to laugh.

"Sorry," she said. "I don't know why I'm laughing. I'm sorry. Taylor didn't have a boyfriend. She wasn't into men if you know what I mean."

"I see," Bridge said. "What about a girlfriend then? Did she ever talk about a girlfriend?"

"No. She didn't talk about much other than the shop."

"Taylor used to make some of the products sold in the shop, didn't she?" DC Moore said.

"Quite a lot of it," Tanya said. "She was always coming up with new ideas for the dreamcatchers. She loved those dreamcatchers."

"Did she like to paint?" Bridge said.

"I think that's what she did at Uni - art."

"Can you remember her ever mentioning an artist's workshop? It started on a Facebook group – *Art4Fun*. Does that ring a bell?"

Another shake of the head.

"OK," Bridge said. "I'd like you to talk me through what happened today. Taylor was alone in the shop when she was attacked. Where were you?"

"I take my lunch break between twelve and one," Vanya said. "It was a nice day, so I bought a sandwich and went to the Museum Gardens to eat it."

"And Taylor remained in the shop?" DC Moore said.

"She never leaves it. Spends her lunch break making stuff. She was really keen to make a start on some new dreamcatchers."

Bridge remembered the pendant around Paula Burton's neck.

"You've mentioned the dreamcatchers more than once," he said. "Was Taylor well known for them?"

"They're her signature product," Vanya said.

"So it's safe to say quite a few people were aware of her work?" DC Moore said.

"I suppose so."

"When you leave for lunch," Bridge said. "Does Taylor keep the shop open?"

"Not anymore," Vanya said. "She used to, but she kept getting distracted by customers."

"So Energy Emporium is closed between twelve and one every day?"

"That's right."

"How do the customers who are not aware of this know?"

"There's a sign on the door," Vanya said. "*Closed for lunch.*"

"Is the shop locked during that time?"

Vanya's eyes started to dart about again. Bridge looked at her and frowned.

"Is something wrong?"

"I think I forgot to lock the door when I went on lunch."

"Has that happened before?" DC Moore asked her.

"Sometimes."

"I presume you have a key for the shop then?" Bridge said.

"No. It's got one of those locks that automatically lock when you flip the button down. I forgot to do it today."

"How do you get back inside the shop?" DC Moore said.

"Taylor lets me back in. I don't think she trusted me with a key."

"We're almost finished," Bridge said. "Do you have many regulars at the shop? People who keep coming back?"

"I suppose so," Vanya said.

"Could you perhaps make a list of them?"

"What for? Do you think one of our customers did that to her?"

"If you could just think about that list," DC Moore said.

"I can't think about anything right now."

"That's fine." Bridge took out one of his cards and gave it to her. "You can send it to the email address on there. Can you think of anyone who struck you as suspicious hanging around the shop recently?"

"What do you mean?"

"Someone who lingered longer than was reasonable inside the shop," Bridge said.

"Not that I remember," Vanya said. "Although I'm not very observant. Taylor was the one with the suspicious mind."

Bridge got to his feet. "I think that's all for now."

"What do you think will happen to the shop?" Vanya said.

"I really don't know," Bridge said. "If you could make that list sometime today, I would appreciate it."

CHAPTER THIRTY SEVEN

After speaking once more to the family and friends of the other victims the team realised that they didn't have much to write home about. Neither Patti Apple nor Lionel Grange could shed any more light on why their partners had to die. They did get something positive from a search of Paula Burton's flat though. It was a flyer advertising portrait painting. The number at the bottom of the advert was the same one they found on Jennifer Cole's phone.

"This is definitely how he did it," Smith decided.

He was drinking a cup of coffee in the canteen. Bridge and DC Moore were sitting at the table with him.

"It doesn't really help us though, does it?" DC Moore said. "We already know that the mobile number doesn't exist anymore, and it wasn't registered to anyone."

"Where did these women get the flyers?" Smith said.

"What difference does it make?" Bridge said. "The flyers are a dead end."

"Not necessarily," Smith argued. "If we can get some idea of where the victims saw the adverts, we might get lucky and find out who put them there."

"That is a hell of a long shot," DC Moore said.

"Long shots sometimes hit the target, Harry. Where would someone advertise portrait painting?"

"We've trawled the art galleries and museums," Bridge reminded him.

"But we were focused only on the paintings," Smith said. "We only asked if the style of the painting was familiar. We didn't mention anything about the flyers."

"I suppose it's worth a try," DC Moore said.

Smith gazed out of the window at the Minster in the distance. "Someone out there knows something that will point us in the direction of *The Painter*.

We just need to find the right person to speak to."

"In a city with a population of a hundred and forty thousand?" Bridge said. "We've got a lot of people to get through."

"What did the assistant from the hippy shop have to say?" Smith said.

"It's a new-age shop, Sarge," DC Moore corrected. "*Hippy* is so last century."

"Same thing. What do we know about Taylor Jenkins?"

"She studied art," Bridge said. "And she was well known for her dreamcatchers."

"*The Painter* was aware of them," Smith said. "He painted a pendant of one on the portrait of Paula Burton. Hold on…"

"What is it?" DC Moore said.

"Was Paula actually wearing a necklace with a pendant?"

A short phone call to Billie Jones confirmed that she wasn't. There was a chain around her neck but that's all it was – a simple gold chain.

"Fuck it," Smith said. "We dropped the ball there."

"It wouldn't have made any difference, mate," Bridge said and patted him on the shoulder. "The connection between the dreamcatcher and Taylor Jenkins was too flimsy. It would have been impossible to tie the two together from a simple necklace pendant."

"I suppose you're right. We don't know anything, do we?"

"We've still got Henry Harvey," DC Moore said.

"No we don't. The man has disappeared into thin air. All we know is that all the victims were members of some Facebook art group. None of their family and friends remember anything about the workshops, and as far as we're aware none of the victims were acquainted outside of that group. Did the assistant tell you anything else about Taylor Jenkins?"

"She had a suspicious nature," Bridge said. "She didn't trust anyone."

"Vanya wasn't allowed a key to the shop," DC Moore remembered. "And she said Taylor would watch the customers closely in case they stole something."

"What about CCTV?" Smith said. "If she was so paranoid about stock growing feet, surely she would put up cameras."

"Nothing," Bridge said.

"Don't you think that's odd?"

"I suppose it is, but it's not going to help us, is it?"

Whitton came in with Baldwin. They joined Smith, Bridge and DC Moore at the table.

"The DI thinks we should call it a day," Whitton said.

"I won't argue with that," Bridge said.

"We're missing something important," Smith said.

"Aren't we always?" DC Moore said.

"*The Painter* only used the ruse of the portrait painting on two of them. Jennifer Cole and Paula Burton were lured to their deaths because of those flyers but Davina Hawkins and Taylor Jenkins weren't. And the way that Taylor was killed suggested she knew who was attacking her, but Davina's reaction in the CCTV footage when the courier stood on her doorstep means either she didn't know the person, or she did and she felt threatened by them."

"Where are you going with this?" Whitton asked.

"Round and round in circles," Smith said and rubbed his eyes. "There isn't one single similarity between any of the murders. He drugs two of them, but he doesn't bother with the other two. He killed two of them at home but the others were carried out somewhere else."

"He's adaptable," Bridge said.

"And he's done his homework," Smith said. "He has contingency plans in place."

He stopped there and raised his eyes, so they were focused on the lights in the ceiling.

"What is it?" Whitton said.

"What's what?" Smith lowered his eyes.

"You do that when you've had one of your lightbulb moments."

Smith grinned at her. "Do I?"

"Yes, you do. Your eyes shift in their sockets."

"How did he know Jennifer and Paula would see the flyers?"

"I see what you mean," Bridge said. "For his plan to work – in order to lure them with the promise of getting their portraits painted, he needed them to pick up the flyers in the first place."

"I don't think they were on display anywhere," Smith decided.

"Are you saying they were personally handed to the women?" DC Moore said.

"Something like that. They could have been hand delivered through their letterboxes."

"He would be running the risk of their partners finding them," Bridge pointed out.

"Paula Burton lived alone, and Jennifer Cole's partner worked full time. He knows everything about them, and at the risk of sounding like a stuck record, this one leaves nothing to chance."

"He didn't risk posting a flyer through Davina Hawkins' letterbox because he knew about the CCTV across the road," DC Moore said.

"And he planned to attack Taylor Jenkins at her shop all along," Whitton added. "Because he knew the assistant left the shop at lunchtime."

"He knows they're all interested in art because they all attended the workshops," Bridge joined in.

"But who the hell is he?" Smith said.

DC King's arrival interrupted their train of thought.

"Henry Harvey has been found."

"Where is he?" Smith asked.

"We were unable to find him because he's been in hospital. He was involved in a hit and run yesterday, and he's been in hospital ever since."
"How serious is it?" Bridge said.
"A few broken bones," DC King said. "But he's conscious and according to the doctors he's well enough to answer a few questions."

CHAPTER THIRTY EIGHT

Henry Harvey didn't look like someone who had recently been involved in a hit and run. The only telltale sign was the brace around his neck. His face didn't have a scratch on it, and his eyes were bright. Smith and Whitton had been told by one of the doctors that Henry had suffered a few broken ribs. The neck brace was merely a precaution. Even though they knew Henry wasn't *The Painter* – he was in hospital at the time Taylor Jenkins was killed, they still had a few questions they needed him to answer.

Smith pulled up a couple of chairs and he and Whitton sat down next to the bed.
"How are you feeling?" Smith asked.
"Like I've been hit by a bus," Henry said.
He laughed but the grimace on his face told Smith it was a bad idea.
"What happened?" Whitton said.
"It was probably my own fault. I was on my way home from the pub and I only saw the car when it was too late. I crossed without looking, so I don't understand why he didn't stop afterwards. I would have admitted it was my fault."
"Has someone been to see you to take a statement?" Smith said.
Henry nodded. "For what it's worth. It was dark and I can't really remember the car or the driver. The docs reckon I'll be right as rain in no time anyway. I suppose I should count myself lucky. A sprained ankle and a few broken ribs isn't too bad."
"Broken ribs are not pleasant," Smith said. "I should know."
A nurse came in and asked Henry if he needed any painkillers. Henry thanked him and said he didn't.
"You're not here about the hit and run, are you?" he said when the nurse had left the room.

"No," Smith confirmed. "I want to know why you lied to me the last time we spoke."

"I don't remember lying to you."

"I asked you if you knew Jennifer Cole and Davina Hawkins and you denied any knowledge of knowing them."

"I don't know them," Henry said.

"I don't believe you. Does a Facebook group called *Art4Fun* ring any bells?"

"OK," Henry said. "I might have told a little white lie. I was acquainted with them, but that was ages ago."

"Why did you pretend you didn't know who they were?" Whitton said.

"Because I didn't want any trouble."

"Why would you think you'd be in trouble?" Smith said.

"Because I knew about their murders. I read about it on social media. I didn't want the hassle of the police being on my back."

"Usually, when someone lies to us during an investigation, we start to smell something *off*," Smith said. "But in your case, all I can smell is the stench of antiseptic."

A different nurse came in. She checked the level of the drip next to the bed and left without saying a word.

"I hate hospitals," Henry said. "They never give you any peace to help you get better."

"We're on the same page there," Smith said. "What can you tell us about the Facebook group?"

"What is it you want to know?"

"What made you join the group?" Whitton asked.

"It seemed like a good idea at the time," Henry said.

"Go on," Smith said.

"I'd been dabbling with art for a while, and I wondered if I might be able to make some money out of it. I saw the group and I thought, why not? It might pay to make friends with some other artists and show a few of my paintings."

"Did you display your art on the group?" Whitton said.

"Just the once," Henry said. "I got a few comments about how I might be able to improve but it was pretty clear I was never going to be the next Picasso. Most of the people were just being polite."

"There were some workshops here in York," Smith said. "They were advertised on the group. Did you attend any of these?"

"I did."

"What happened at these workshops?" Whitton said.

"The first one was a waste of time from an art perspective. I remember it was more of a night out. A few drinks and maybe the odd mention of a painting or two."

"And you didn't go to any more after that?" Smith said.

"What makes you say that?"

"You said the initial one was a waste of time."

"From an art perspective," Henry repeated.

"What other perspective is there at an art workshop?" Whitton wondered.

"Let's just say I liked what I saw," Henry said.

"Could you please stop talking in riddles," Smith said. "We don't want to be here all night."

"A group of young women," Henry said. "Arty types. Use your imagination."

"You carried on attending the workshops because you thought you might get lucky with one of the women there?" Smith said.

"Why not? I'm a single bloke – there's no harm in trying."

"Were there any other men besides yourself at these workshops?" Whitton said.

"None," Henry said. "That's why I reckoned the odds were definitely in my favour. Four women and one man. Even the most pig-ugly, socially challenged bloke would have stood a chance with odds like that."

"And did you get lucky?" Smith said.

Henry started to laugh again. He winced and grabbed hold of his ribs. "The docs warned me about laughing."

"Can I ask you what you find so amusing?" Smith said.

"You asked me if I got lucky," Henry said. "Brad Pitt wouldn't have stood a chance with that lot."

"Why is that?" Whitton said.

"Because what I had to offer wasn't what they were interested in, if you know what I mean."

"Your natural charm and sophistication?" Smith guessed.

"My maleness," Henry said. "Whatever you want to call it. Those women weren't interested in men. Do I have to draw you a picture?"

"That won't be necessary," Whitton said.

"We'll leave you in peace," Smith said. "Get well soon."

CHAPTER THIRTY NINE

"What a horrible man," Whitton said.

They'd gone straight home from the hospital. Smith handed her a beer.

"And we're back to square one," he said.

He drained half of his beer in one go.

"He's not *The Painter*," Whitton said. "He was in hospital when Taylor Jenkins was killed. I don't know where to look now."

"I do," Smith said.

He walked over to the freezer and opened it.

"I'm hungry, and what I'm looking at right now doesn't look very appetising."

"We can't live on takeaways," Whitton said.

"The kids won't complain."

"The kids wouldn't know good food if it slapped them in the face."

A knock on the door solved their problem. When Smith opened it Shelia Rogers was standing there with her daughter. Shelia had a casserole dish in her hands. Smith invited them in, and they followed him to the kitchen.

"Shelia has brought us some food," Smith told Whitton.

"I made a toad in the hole," Sheila said. "I made enough for all of us. I'd rather me and Fran weren't home alone."

"Sounds like a fair deal to me," Smith said. "You provide the food, and we do the dishes."

"I don't mean to intrude."

"You're not, Sheila," Whitton said. "It sounds like a great idea. Do you want something to drink?"

"We've got beer or beer," Smith said. "Although I think there's half a bottle of Jack Daniel's somewhere."

"I've got some wine next door," Sheila said. "I'll go and grab a couple of bottles. Are you sure this is OK?"

"It's more than OK," Smith told her. "We were just talking about what we were going to eat tonight. Do you want me to come with you?"

Sheila laughed. "I'm sure I'll be fine. I'm only popping next door. Where did Fran go?"

Her whole demeanour changed. Her eyes grew wide and she scanned the room for her daughter.

"It's fine," Whitton said. "She went upstairs to Laura's room."

"I'll go and get that wine then."

"She's terrified," Whitton said when she'd gone.

"She has good reason to be," Smith said. "The boss said he'd organise some extra patrols in the area, but I don't think that's enough to put her mind at ease."

"Do you really think she's in danger?"

"She shouldn't be," Smith said. "She only went to one of the art workshops, but it's possible *The Painter* has her on his list. Nothing that psycho has done so far has made any logical sense. I'm going out for a smoke."

He went outside to the back garden. He lit a cigarette and looked over the fence to Sheila Rogers' house. The place was in darkness. Smith made a mental note to tell her to switch on a few lights to make it look like someone was home. The conversation with Henry Harvey came back to him. He didn't think the fact that the women in the group were all attracted to women was significant. How could it be? He was running out of ideas. They'd reached the point in the investigation where they'd used up all their leads. As far as Smith was concerned there wasn't anything else to look into, and he knew from experience that when they reached that stage often things got ugly. Frustration caused the team to turn on one another and things were said that couldn't be unsaid.

Sheila Rogers hadn't returned when Smith went back inside. He asked Whitton what was taking her so long.

"Perhaps she forgot where she put the wine," she said.

"The house is pitch black," Smith said. "She should know to leave a few lights on when she goes out."

Lucy came into the kitchen with Andrew in her arms. She passed him to Whitton, and she raised him up into the air.

"Who's my big boy?"

"He weighs a ton," Smith said.

"He's a healthy weight according to the chart," Lucy said. "What's for tea?"

"Sheila brought over a toad in the hole," Whitton said. "She just popped next door to pick up some wine."

"She should have been back by now," Smith said. "I'm going to go and see what's wrong."

It was unnecessary. Sheila came back in with two bottles of wine. She placed them on the sideboard and explained what took her so long.

"I think I might need more than the wine tonight. I got a phone call while I was next door. It was my solicitor. He called me on a Sunday evening to tell me my bastard of an ex has disappeared off the face of the earth. He hasn't paid what he's supposed to pay according to the terms of the divorce for the last few months, and it looks like that's now a permanent arrangement."

"Surely your solicitor can find him and make him pay," Smith said.

"He legged it to Canada," Sheila said. "I suppose it's a big enough place to get lost in."

"I'm sorry, Sheila," Whitton said.

"I'm not. Good riddance to him. I don't want his money anyway."

"What's for tea?" It was Laura.

She and Fran were standing in the doorway.

"I'll open the wine," Smith said. "Laura, you and Fran can put out the knives and forks."

Twenty minutes later, there wasn't a scrap of food left. The toad in the hole had gone down well and the dogs were not impressed. Theakston and Fred were both staring at the contents of their food bowls as though they were full of something radioactive.

"It's dog food," Smith told them. "Last time I looked, you were both dogs."

Darren had offered to wash the dishes and, after a lengthy discussion on ulterior motives Smith was satisfied that the teenage boy didn't have one. Darren was offering because he wanted to help out. When he was finished, he and Lucy went upstairs to put Andrew to bed.

"That food was delicious," Smith said. "I'm stuffed."
He took another beer out of the fridge.
"Not stuffed enough to be able to fit some more beer in," Whitton said.
"It's impossible to be that stuffed."
"Can I ask you something?" Sheila said.
Whitton topped up their wine glasses. "Of course."
"This may sound a bit morbid, but will you hear me out?"
"I don't like the sound of this," Smith said. "Can I be excused? Can I go outside for a smoke?"
"No," Whitton said. "Go on, Sheila."
"The phone call from the solicitor got me thinking," Sheila said. "It made me think about what would happen to Fran if anything happened to me."
"Nothing is going to happen to you," Smith said.
"You never know. I'm all she has left. I'm the only person Fran has. Her dad has made it quite clear he's not interested, my parents are both dead, and I've nobody else who could take her in if something happened to me."
"Nothing is going to happen, Sheila," Smith said once more.
"Would you be prepared to have her?"

Smith almost spat out his beer. "What?"

"In the event of something happening to me, would you be willing to look after Fran? She loves all of you, and I know you'll take care of her."

"That's a big ask, Sheila," Whitton said.

"And it's hypothetical," Smith added. "You're going to be around to walk that little girl down the aisle one day. You've still got a long life ahead of you."

"I need to know," Sheila said. "Please – it would put my mind at rest."

"Alright then," Smith said. "Anything happens to you - Fran can come and live with us."

He couldn't see Whitton's facial expression, but he could sense it. He could feel her eyes burning into the back of his head. It was definitely time to smoke that cigarette now.

CHAPTER FORTY

Whitton was already up when Smith woke the next day. Her side of the bed was cold, and he wondered if that was a reflection of her mood. They hadn't spoken a word since Smith had offered to take Sheila Rogers' daughter in, in the event of Sheila's death. Smith had tried to justify it by explaining that it was highly unlikely that anything would happen to Sheila, but Whitton hadn't been listening. She'd headed upstairs to bed as soon as Sheila and Fran had gone, and Smith wondered what the reception was going to be like when he went downstairs.

Whitton was sitting at the table in the kitchen, looking at something on her phone. Smith placed his hand on her shoulders. She didn't shake them off and Smith decided this was a good start.

"I'm sorry about what I promised Sheila."

"No," Whitton said. "I'm sorry about how I reacted. It just came as a bit of a shock."

"It's not going to happen," Smith said. "Nothing is going to happen to Sheila."

"You're right. What made you make an offer like that?"

"I have no idea," Smith said. "I guess I'm just a sucker for a sob story. Where are the kids?"

"Where do you think? It's Monday morning, and it's the school holidays. Lucy and Darren will get up when Andrew demands it, but I haven't heard a peep out of him, so I think they're making the most of it."

"We're going to make some progress today," Smith said.

"Do you really believe that?" Whitton said.

"I have to believe it."

"It's possible that he's finished you know. There was no painting at the scene of Taylor Jenkins' murder, so it could mean that he's completed what he set out to do."

"I sincerely hope so," Smith said. "I was awake half the night thinking about his motivation, and I don't think these women were killed out of hatred."

"He certainly didn't gain financially from their deaths," Whitton said. "And I can't see how it could be about revenge. What other motives are there? Jealousy? What could he possibly envy in those four women? What else is there?"

"Love," Smith said. "I think this is all about love."

* * *

The Painter had only known true love once. And when it happened it was an all-encompassing, truly extraordinary thing. It took over body and soul, and it was always there. Day and night it caressed and warmed from the inside out.

There was only one canvas left. The others were strewn all over the floor, in various stages of completion. This piece had to be done right. Taylor Jenkins wasn't expecting to die yesterday, and *The Painter* needed to get that across in the painting. The crystals on the shelves behind her were exquisite, and it was going to take some time to recreate them on the canvas.

The Painter's gaze shifted from the image of the dead woman on the screen to the artwork on the wall behind it. This piece hadn't been created out of love. There was no love in the entwined bodies of the women on the canvas. With grimaces of ecstasy on their faces and limbs entwined in impossible ways, this was not *The Painter's* version of love. These naked forms were something born of depravity.

It really was an exceptional piece, nevertheless – one which changed depending on the angle it was viewed from. Often *The Painter* would glance at it from the side and the women would appear to dance. Legs and arms would move in unnatural ways. Other times their faces would morph into something devilish. Their eyes would promise malice. Once, one of them had grown horns.

Taylor Jenkins would be painted with horns sprouting from her head, *The Painter* decided. Horns and a reptile's tail.

"A tail for Taylor."

The voice belonged to someone else.

The paint on the palette had started to dry. *The Painter* dabbed some water onto it and added some more yellow. This would be used to highlight the edges of the crystals. Taylor Jenkins would be painted on afterwards.

An hour later the background was done and *The Painter* was happy with it. One of the crystals resembled a snake's open mouth and this hadn't been intentional. The first brushstroke of what would become the dead woman was applied to the canvas. It was going to take some time to complete this part of the painting, but time was something *The Painter* had in abundance.

Detective Smith wasn't going to view this piece on the screen of a phone, *The Painter* decided. He wasn't going to see this for the first time on a laptop – that would be unfair to both Smith and to Taylor Jenkins. This had to be seen in its purest form. He would be gifted the painting as soon as it was completed.

CHAPTER FORTY ONE

"There's a woman here to speak to you."
Baldwin pounced on Smith the moment he walked through the doors of the station.
"Who is she?" he asked.
"Her name is Samantha Roland and she said she has some information about the *Art4Fun* workshops."
"Where is she?"
"I suggested she wait in the canteen," Baldwin said. "I told her you wouldn't be long."
"I'll go straight up. Thanks, Baldwin."

Samantha Rowland was a pretty woman who looked to be in her mid-thirties. Her green eyes were framed by dark red glasses. Her face was tanned, and Smith wondered if she'd recently spent some time abroad. She didn't get that tan in York. She was sitting in Smith's usual seat by the window, sketching something on a small notepad.
"What are you drawing?" Smith asked her.
"You have a stunning view from up here."
Samantha showed him the notepad. On it was a pencil drawing of the buildings in the distance. The spires of the Minster were yet to be drawn.
"That's really good," Smith said. "We can talk in my office. We won't get disturbed there. Can I offer you something to drink?"
"The lovely PC at the front desk already gave me some coffee."

Smith asked Samantha to take a seat and closed the door to his office. He sat down opposite her. "What is it you want to talk to me about?"
"I came here as soon as I heard about the dead women."
Smith was all ears. He thought this was a really strange thing to say.
"Could you explain what you mean by that?" he said.

"I knew them," Samantha said. "I knew all of them."

"Why is it you've only just heard about the murders? The news and social media have consisted of very little else for days."

"I've been away. I run an artist's retreat in Gozo, Malta the same time every year."

"What does this retreat entail?" Smith said.

"Isolation. That's why I chose Gozo. My students are free to express themselves without distraction. For a week there is no outside influence to muddy the creative process. No phones, and no Internet."

"It sounds liberating."

"It is," Samantha said. "You should give it a try sometime. Anything goes at these retreats. The artists there are able to paint at will. They can create their art stark naked if that's what inspires them."

"I don't think I'd be able to do that," Smith said.

"Are you an artist?"

"Not at all. I've played guitar for twenty odd years, but that's as far as anything creative goes with me."

"Then you are an artist."

"How is it that you know these women?" Smith asked.

"I was called upon to tutor the artists at the *Art4Fun* workshops."

"When was this?"

"May 2018."

"You sound very convinced about the date," Smith said.

"It was May 2018. I checked before I came here."

"What happened at these workshops?" Smith said. "I believe there were only a few artists there."

"That's right. I remember six people signed up, but one of them didn't return after the first one."

Sheila Roberts, Smith thought.

"I've spoken to someone who was at one of the workshops," he said. "She was the one who only went once, and she said nothing much was achieved in the initial one."

"That was intentional," Samantha told him. "These things are personal, and it's essential that the people involved are comfortable with one another. The first workshop was more of a *get-to-know* sort of thing. A few drinks to ease the inhibitions. The partners of the artists were welcome to come along to that one too."

"I see," Smith said. "But the others were different?"

"There were only four more workshops. Things seemed to take a different turn after the third one and I decided to do one more, and then call it a day. The attention soon fell away from the subject matter."

"Where did it go?" Smith said. "What changed?"

"It became less about art when some of the students started developing feelings for some of the others."

"There was only one man there, wasn't there?" Smith said. "Henry Harvey."

"Henry," Samantha smiled. "He was rather memorable."

"Was he any good?"

"All art is subjective. What appeals to one person may be abhorrent to another, but I can tell you that Henry was a mediocre artist. And it was quite clear that his interest in the workshops was not art related."

"He went there for the women."

There was a knock at the door and PC Griffin came inside.

"Not now," Smith told him.

"I might have found something, Sarge," PC Griffin said.

"I said not now. I'm busy with something at the moment."

PC Griffin nodded and left them to it.

"Sorry about that," Smith said. "Did you get to know any of the women at the workshops well? In a personal capacity I mean."

"Our relationship was exclusively workshop related," Samantha said.

"You said you were called upon to tutor the workshops," Smith said. "Who asked you to do that?"

"It was someone on the Facebook group. Nicola Gregg, I think her name was. We discussed it via Messenger, and she organised the venue and paid my fee into my bank account."

"Did she ever attend any of the workshops?"

"No," Samantha said.

"Didn't you think that was odd? The woman who arranged the workshops didn't come to any of them?"

"I didn't give it a second thought. It wasn't a scam – I was paid what I asked, and the women who were supposed to be there, were there."

"How long have you been painting?" Smith said.

"As long as I can remember," Samantha said. "Ever since I was a little girl, I've been creating art on whatever surface I could find."

"Would you consider yourself an expert then?"

"I really don't know how to answer that."

"You'd know better than most whether a piece of art was done by someone who knows what they're doing," Smith rephrased the question.

"As I said, all art is subjective. It's said that art reflects life, but that reflection is only a reflection as the artist perceives it. It's a debate that we could spend days discussing, but I'm sure you don't have days."

"No," Smith confirmed. "I don't. Would you be able to recognise a style of painting you'd seen before?"

"Probably."

"Do you need to be anywhere today?"

"I was planning on getting some rest," Samantha said. "The retreat was rather draining, and I was going to take a couple of days to unwind after it."

"I would really like you to help me."

"In what way?"

Smith told her.

"I'll have to get it authorised first," he added. "But I can't see it being a problem."

CHAPTER FORTY TWO

"Are you out of your fucking mind?"
Smith was lost for words. He'd known DI Smyth for quite a while now and he'd rarely heard him swear.
"Are you alright, boss?" he found his voice.
"I'm fine," DI Smyth said. "It appears that it's you we need to be worried about. What you've just suggested are the words of a madman."
"She can help us."
"You can't seriously expect me to authorise this. You want to let a complete stranger take a look at confidential evidence in a multiple murder investigation."
"She's not a total stranger," Smith argued. "I reckon I've got to know her pretty well in the past hour. And she was the one who headed up the *Art4Fun* workshops. She can help us."
"How are we to know she isn't just some nutjob getting a kick out of it?"
"Because I didn't get that impression. She's the real deal, boss. She was in charge of those workshops, and she might be able to tell us something about the paintings we haven't spotted because we know fuck all about art. What have we got to lose?"
"Our jobs," DI Smyth said. "For starters. How do we know she's not going to go running to the press with this. Have you considered that?"
"I don't believe she will. She was reluctant when I asked her for help. She's just come back from a retreat in Gozo, and she told me she'd rather go home to get some rest. Why would she do that if she was planning on selling her story to the highest bidder. You have to trust me on this."

DI Smyth ran his hands through his hair. "Do you know what?"
"What's that, boss?"
"Before I met you, I had a full head of hair, and now it's falling out in

clumps."

"It suits you. Well?"

"Don't let me regret this," DI Smyth said.

"I wouldn't dream of it."

"And I want you to make it absolutely clear to this woman what will happen if anything she's shown is leaked to the press."

"I'll give her the perversion of justice, interfering in the course of an investigation bullshit," Smith promised. "You won't regret this."

"I already am regretting it."

* * *

"Do you want me to drive?" Samantha Rowland asked.

It was the third time the car had jumped forwards abruptly. Smith had borrowed Whitton's car to take Samantha to the New Forensics Building.

"I'm not used to the brakes on this thing," he explained. "The ones on my old Sierra aren't so sensitive."

"Perhaps if you slowed down a bit you wouldn't have to slam on the brakes so hard," Samantha suggested.

Smith didn't realise he was speeding but the gauge in front of him told him was ten miles per hour over the limit.

"And my old Ford lets me know when I'm going too fast. The engine makes funny noises. God, I miss that car."

They made it to the New Forensics Building without incident and Samantha told Smith she would call a taxi to take her home when they were finished. Smith had warned Webber that they were coming, and the Head of Forensics had informed him he wouldn't be there. He was still busy inside Energy Emporium. Smith had been surprised. He thought the forensics team had finished in the new age shop, but Webber wanted to take another look. He was sure they'd overlooked something yesterday and he wanted to go over the murder scene again in peace.

Billie Jones was there to meet them. Smith introduced her to Samantha Roland and Billie led them upstairs to where the paintings were being kept. Smith had suggested he show the artist the photographs of the paintings but Samantha told him she would prefer to view the originals. A photograph wouldn't give her a detailed idea of what was going through the painter's mind when he painted it – she explained that she needed to examine the brushstrokes and the emotion displayed in the painting.

"I have to warn you," Smith said. "This is probably going to be upsetting for you. You were acquainted with the women in the paintings and some of them are incredibly graphic."

"I'll bear that in mind," Samantha said. "It's important that I view them in the order they were painted."

"Why is that?"

"To look at the progression."

"You sound like you've done this kind of thing before," Smith said.

"I assure you I haven't. Shall we do this?"

Billie opened the door and led them to where the painting of Jennifer Cole was on display.

"This was the first one," Smith told Samantha.

"I'll leave you to it," Billie said and walked back out of the room.

"This was painted in stages," Samantha said.

"That part we did manage to figure out," Smith said.

"The work behind her is Barnard's *Maze of Chaos*."

"We worked that out too."

"Barnard's piece is replicated in watercolour," Samantha said. "But Jennifer was painted using oil-based paint. It's generally frowned upon to combine the two. Your painter was in a hurry."

"Can you explain what you mean by that?"

"Water-based paint dries quickly, whereas oil-based materials can take days, even weeks to completely dry. The background was important to this artist, but he needed it finished quickly."

Smith didn't tell her how right she was about the background. Samantha Rowland was already privy to more information than she should be.

"The artist is very good," he said.

Samantha nodded. "He's right-handed. The strokes don't lie. And they're also telling me another story. The subject was close to this artist – more than close. There is love in the brushstrokes on this canvas."

"We believe she knew the painter," Smith confirmed.

"She knew him very well."

"Is there anything else you can see?" Smith asked.

"The eyes were painted last."

"How can you tell?"

"I know a thing or two about faces," Samantha said. "Look at me."

"What?"

"Look at me. Look right at me and smile."

Smith humoured her with his best toothy grin.

"The shape of your lips is telling me that you're smiling," Samantha said.

"That's because I am," Smith said.

"And your eyes are telling the same story. So much actually, that I no longer need to look at your mouth. The smile in Jennifer's eyes is at odds with the shape of her mouth. Her eyes are observing someone she loves deeply, but the arc of her mouth is something you'd expect to see when someone has told you a joke that wasn't particularly funny, but you smiled anyway, out of obligation."

"What does it mean though?" Smith asked.

"Her eyes were definitely painted like that for a reason. I'd guess that the artist wanted to portray deep, heartfelt love in those eyes."

"Love for the painter?"

"Maybe. It is also possible that a modicum of artistic license was used."
"He painted her eyes how he wanted them to look back at him?"
"Could be. Shall we look at the others?"

CHAPTER FORTY THREE

Grant Webber wasn't sure what he was expecting to find inside Energy Emporium, but he sensed there was something they had missed yesterday. He did wonder if it could be all inside his head. The similarities of these murders to the way in which he lost the only woman he'd ever truly loved had brought everything back to him, and it was possible his desire to be utterly alone at a crime scene was somehow related to that. Was he hoping to remember her in this morbid way? Did he think he would bring her closer to him like this?

He pushed his thoughts aside and focused on the interior of the shop. He had to admit that he didn't really know what most of the products on offer were. There were stones and crystals of all shapes and colours on display opposite the cash desk. Taylor Jenkins' body had been taken away, but the evidence of what happened to her was very apparent. Her blood had seeped into the thick pile of the carpet, and Webber knew it would be almost impossible to clean it. He wondered why a shop had been fitted with such luxurious carpet.

There was a Feng Sui display next to the cash desk. Webber had heard of the ancient Chinese practice, but he wasn't familiar with the principles. It was something related to energy if he recalled, and this tied in with the name of the shop. He had to admit that *Energy Emporium* really was a catchy name.

"What am I looking for?" he asked nobody in particular.

He took out his phone and took some photographs of where Taylor Jenkins had fallen. Billie Jones had measured the initial arterial spurt and it had been an impressive three metres. Webber had seen longer spurts, but this one was close to the record. He knew from experience that when they came across something like that it was because the victim's heart had been beating unusually quickly when the carotids were severed.

"What was going through your mind before he did this to you?"

He wasn't sure why he asked this. Webber was a man of science and he focused on that science without exception. He wondered whether Billie Jones had been right. Was this investigation starting to affect him? Should he take her advice and take a step back?

He took some more photographs. This time he concentrated on the area around the cash desk and the part of the shop closest to the door. Some of Taylor Jenkins' blood had landed on the cash register. The plastic till would be difficult to clean. More blood had splashed onto the wall behind the counter.

Webber picked up one of the healing crystals without realising. It was black and shiny. The label stuck to the bottom told him it was *Obsidian* and it claimed to help process emotions and aid in letting go. It was priced at nine pounds. He wondered whether people actually believed in the healing power of crystals. He examined the black rock and put it in his pocket. He took out his wallet, removed a ten-pound note and stuffed it in the gap underneath the cash register.

There were a few African masks on display on the wall behind the counter. A sign had been put up informing customers that they weren't for sale. Webber wondered why that was. He took a closer look at the masks and one in particular caught his attention. It was an ebony mask, and the head was elongated. The nose sprouted from the forehead and the eyes were blank holes. The upturned mouth gave it a mournful aspect. It really was a morbid creation, but Webber found himself drawn to it. He couldn't explain why. Spots of Taylor Jenkins' blood had landed on it. Webber took a couple of photographs of it for no particular reason.

He was getting side-tracked. He stepped towards the display of healing crystals. Taylor Jenkins had been standing with her back to these when she was attacked. Her neck was slashed two times in quick succession. Webber mimicked this with an imaginary knife.

"Right to left first," he said. "Then left to right."

He deduced that the killer was right-handed for what it was worth.

"That rules out ten percent of the population then."

He wasn't sure what else to look for. Billie Jones had documented the scene in her usual exemplary manner, and Webber knew she wouldn't have missed anything, so what had brought him back here? He didn't have an answer to that. He gripped the Obsidian in his pocket and left the shop.

* * *

"Where did DS Smith go?" PC Griffin asked Baldwin at the front desk.

"He went to the New Forensics Building," she told him. "He wanted to show the paintings to an expert."

"When will he be back?"

"When he's finished."

"There's no need to be sarcastic," PC Griffin said.

"I was stating a fact. What do you need him for?"

"I might have found something. I'll take it to the DI."

He made his way to DI Smyth's office. The door was wide open, so he went straight in. DI Smyth was talking to someone on the phone. He held up a hand to tell PC Griffin to let him finish. From the snippets he heard he guessed that DI Smyth was talking to Smith.

He ended the call. "What is it?"

"I think I've found something, sir," PC Griffin told him.

"Take a seat."

"DS Smith suggested we revisit the victims," PC Griffin said. "Look at them in more detail."

"It often helps," DI Smyth said.

"I managed to track down an ex-boyfriend of Paula Burton's. I thought we should be focusing on the lives of the victims at the time the art workshops took place. We're assuming that's the link to their deaths."

"Good thinking."

"Anyway," PC Griffin said. "I did a bit of asking around, and I found out that Paula was seeing a man by the name of James Draper back in 2018. He was easy enough to find. I spoke to him and asked about the workshops, and he told me something interesting. He went to the first workshop with Paula."

"Why is that interesting?" DI Smyth asked.

"Because we didn't consider the partners of the victims before, based on the assumption that this was all about the workshops, but now we know the partners were present we should be looking more closely at them, shouldn't we?"

"You're right. What did Paula's ex have to tell you?"

"He said the partners were invited to take part in the initial workshop. Something to do with making the artists feel more at ease."

"Did he tell you who else was there?" DI Smyth said.

"He couldn't talk much. I caught him at work, but he's agreed to come here when he's finished."

CHAPTER FORTY FOUR

Smith was glad he'd decided to show *The Painter's* artwork to Samantha Rowland. The experienced artist had made some interesting observations when she'd studied the paintings left at the murder scenes. In her opinion the artwork was definitely representative of the emotion of the artist at the time the paintings were completed.

For example, the portrait of Jennifer Cole displayed a lot of love. Samantha was convinced that she and the artist were more than just casually acquainted. Davina Hawkins had been painted exactly as she was found. Her mutilated body had been captured almost clinically, and Samantha didn't think the artist was in anyway emotionally involved with her. Likewise with Paula Purton. Paula's face had been recreated on the canvas beautifully, but Samantha likened it to looking at a photograph of the woman. There was no real passion on display in that painting.

Unfortunately, Samantha couldn't offer any more than that. She didn't recognise anything in the style of the painting, and she didn't think she'd come across the artist before. All she knew for certain was the painter was exceptionally talented, and she imagined they'd received a high level of training at some time.

Smith parked Whitton's car at the station and got out. He lit a cigarette and took out his phone. He wanted to check to see if he'd missed another email from *The Painter*. A glance at his Gmail told him he hadn't. He was beginning to wonder if there would even be any more. They hadn't found a painting at the scene of Taylor Jenkins' murder, and there was only one conclusion to draw from that – *The Painter* was finished.

Smith was halfway through his cigarette when DI Smyth came outside. "Have you got one of those for me?" he nodded to Smith's cigarette.

Smith handed him the pack. "Are you thinking of starting smoking?"

"I gave up years ago," DI Smyth said. "But I get the craving every now and then, especially at times like this."

He lit one and handed the packet back to Smith.

"Samantha Rowland brought up some useful points," Smith told him. "She reckons the artist is incredibly talented, and she wouldn't be surprised if he'd received some training."

"How does that help us?" DI Smyth said.

"She also thinks there were different displays of emotion in all of the paintings. She's convinced that Jennifer Cole was definitely acquainted with the person who painted her."

"The evidence at the scene would suggest that," DI Smyth said. "She definitely knew him."

"It was more than that, boss," Smith said. "Samantha said there was a lot of love in the painting."

"Do you think they were more than friends?"

"It's possible. I think we should speak to Jennifer's girlfriend again. Ask her if she remembers anything unusual about the time of the workshops."

"Such as?"

"All of this stems from something that happened at those workshops," Smith said. "Perhaps Jennifer's girlfriend will remember something from back then. It's worth a shot."

DI Smyth stubbed out his cigarette, half-finished. "PC Griffin has been thinking along the same lines and he might have another lead for us."

Smith sighed. "That bloke is starting to get on my nerves. What has the super sleuth found now?"

"He used his initiative and did some digging into the lives at the time of the workshops. Apparently the first one was open to the partners of the artists too."

"Samantha Rowland mentioned something about it," Smith said. "She said it was designed to make the artists feel more comfortable with one another. Very little was achieved at the first workshop. It was more a tool so the artists could get acquainted. What did Griffin dig up?"

"Paula Burton's boyfriend at the time. It might come to nothing, but he's coming here after work to talk to us. He was at the first workshop so it's possible he can shed some light on what went on at those things."

"Samantha has already told me what went on," Smith said. "They had a few drinks and got to know each other. Nothing more. I suppose I should have pressed her about the subsequent ones."

"Have you received any more emails?" DI Smyth asked.

"Nothing," Smith told him. "I'm starting to wonder if that's because he's finished. When you think about it, it makes sense. There were six people when the workshops started. One of the artists only attended the first one, and one of them is a bloke. He's killed the other four women, so it's highly likely he's completed what he set out to achieve."

"Is Henry Harvey definitely out of the running?"

"He was involved in a hit and run," Smith said. "He was stuck in hospital at the time that Taylor Jenkins was killed."

"What do we know about the hit and run?"

"Henry was crossing the road without looking," Smith said. "A car hit him and drove away. He told me he would have taken the blame. It was his fault."

"Did he have any witnesses to the accident?"

"A report was filed, but I don't think there was anyone else around. What are you thinking?"

"How many hit and runs have you come across?" DI Smyth said.

"Not many."

"Don't you think it's odd that four of the women who attended those workshops are dead," DI Smyth said. "And another man who was there just happens to get hit by a car?"

"Are you suggesting *The Painter* could be involved in Henry's accident?"

"How badly was he hurt?"

"Not badly at all," Smith said. "A sprained ankle and a few broken ribs. It was an accident. If *The Painter* wanted him dead, Henry Harvey would be dead. This is not related to the investigation."

"I'm not suggesting that Mr Harvey was an intended victim," DI Smyth said. "Taylor Jenkins was killed yesterday at around lunchtime."

"And Henry was in hospital at the time," Smith reminded him. "The hit and run happened on Saturday night, and he's been in hospital ever since."

"Do we know that for certain though? Which hospital was he taken to?"

"City Hospital."

"Which happens to be a stone's throw from Energy Emporium. He could have slipped out, killed Taylor and been back within an hour."

"He has a sprained ankle and three broken ribs," Smith said. "He would have been in no condition to kill someone. You're clutching at straws."

"I'm running out of ideas."

"Henry Harvey isn't *The Painter*," Smith said. "Samantha Rowland remembered him well, and she said he was a mediocre artist. The art left at the scenes was done by a very talented painter."

A white car pulled up and a man got out. He looked around and walked over to Smith and DI Smyth.

"Do you work here?"

"We do," Smith confirmed.

"My name is James Draper, and I was asked to come and speak to someone here."

"You're Paula Burton's ex?" DI Smyth said.

"I heard about it on the news."

Smith looked at him closely. He looked to be in his late-twenties, early-thirties and he was completely bald. His scalp was sunburnt, and pieces of skin had peeled off. His brown eyes were narrow and dull. His face had also suffered from too much exposure to the sun and the cheeks were red.

"We can chat in one of the interview rooms," DI Smyth suggested.
"Is it going to take long?" James asked.
"You can never tell," Smith said.
"It's just I promised my wife I would pick up some groceries on the way home. I don't want to miss the shops."
"They'll still be open by the time we're finished," Smith assured him.

CHAPTER FORTY FIVE

"The officer I spoke to said this would just be an informal chat."
James Draper was shocked when Smith went through the motions for the tape. It was clear he hadn't expected to be formally interviewed.
"Don't worry about the recording device," Smith said. "It's just a formality and it saves time later on. You only want to do this once, don't you?"
"I suppose so," James said.
"For the record," DI Smyth said. "Mr Draper came here of his own volition and he is free to leave at any time."

"Can you tell us a bit about Paula Burton?" Smith asked.
"We were together a few years back," James said.
"Can you remember exactly when that was?" DI Smyth said.
"It was 2017 or 2018. No, it was 2018. I remember it because of the World Cup in Russia."
"How long were you in a relationship with Paula?" Smith said.
"About nine months."

"When you spoke to someone here," DI Smyth. "You mentioned something about attending an artist's workshop with her. You couldn't elaborate because you were still at work."
"I'm a foreman at a building site," James said. "We were in the middle of tipping some concrete when I got the call, and the driver of the tipper was making a mess of it. I'm here now aren't I?"
"You are," Smith said. "Tell us about the workshops."
"Paula was really excited about them. She loved drawing, and she'd been on the Facebook group for a while."
"That's the *Art4Fun* group?"
James nodded. "When she heard about the workshops she was over the

moon. They were pretty cheap, and they were all taking place here in York."

"Why did you go with her?" DI Smyth said.

"Because she asked me to," James said. "Why not?"

"What happened at the workshop?" Smith said.

"It wasn't what I expected," James said. "It was basically a group of people getting together for a few drinks."

"I believe that was the intention," DI Smyth said. "It was more of an ice-breaking thing. The later workshops were focused more on the art."

"Can you remember who else was there at the first one?" Smith said.

"I wasn't really interested. There were only a couple of other men if I recall. The rest were women."

"How many people were there in total, would you say?" DI Smyth said.

"About ten of us," James said. "But don't quote me on that."

"OK," Smith said. "I want you to try to remember the two men who were at the workshop. Do the names Henry Harvey and Lionel Grange ring a bell?"

"I think that was their names, yes. I didn't really talk to them much, although I remember now that one of them thought he was God's gift."

Henry Harvey, Smith decided.

"When was the last time you saw Paula?" he said.

"Not since we broke up," James said.

"When was that?"

"Just after the World Cup. That was probably the reason for it. She was pissed off at me for using up all my leave to go and watch the football in Russia."

"I imagine she was," Smith said.

"I wouldn't have missed it for the world. It's not every day you get to watch England play in the semi-final of the World Cup."

"Did they win?" Smith asked.

"Of course they didn't win. That's not the point."

"You broke up with Paula after the football thing," Smith said. "When exactly was that?"

"Not long after I got home from Russia," James said. "It must have been sometime in August 2018."

"And you haven't seen her since?" DI Smyth said.

James scratched at a scab on his head. "No. We called it a day and I haven't seen her since. I was gobsmacked when I read about her murder."

"Did you not see the public appeal we launched?" Smith said. "Paula's face was all over social media and the online news forums."

"I can't say I did. What exactly happened to her?"

Smith avoided the question.

"Can you remember if Paula changed at all while the artists' workshops were going on?" he asked instead.

"In what way?" James said.

"Did you notice if she started acting strangely in any way?" DI Smyth said.

"Not that I recall."

"Did she talk much about the other people at the workshops?" Smith said.

"Sometimes. I was away in Russia for a couple of them, but there is something I remember about the first one she attended when I got back."

"Go on," Smith said.

"She said she wasn't sure if she would be going to any more of them."

"Did she mention why?" DI Smyth said.

"I think some of the artists were starting to make her feel uncomfortable."

"In what way?" Smith said.

"She didn't really elaborate, but I got the impression things had changed. The boundaries had changed."

"Could you explain what you mean by that?" DI Smyth said.

"They were getting bolder in their painting, but some of the stuff Paula showed me bordered on pornography."

"And she wasn't comfortable with that?" Smith said.

"Look," James said. "Paula was no prude, but she wasn't into that kind of stuff. Exhibitionist and expressionist art they called it."

Smith made a mental note to ask Samantha Rowland about this.

"Where were you last Thursday?" he asked James.

"What?"

"Last Thursday," Smith said. "In the afternoon. Where were you?"

"Why are you asking me where I was?"

"Please just answer the question," DI Smyth said.

"I was at work of course."

"You said you work in construction," Smith said.

"I've been working at the site over in Huntington," James said. "We're busy with the new shopping centre there."

"And you were there all day?"

"That's right. You can't think I had anything to do with what happened to Paula. I haven't seen her for a couple of years. I've been working at that site seven days a week for the last month. Why do you think my head looks like it does. Me and the sun don't really get on. And before you ask if I can prove it, the answer's yes."

Smith didn't doubt it. He didn't doubt that James Draper was another person they could tick of the list of suspects. The identity of *The Painter* was still unknown.

CHAPTER FORTY SIX

A couple of hours later the team were still very much in the dark. They'd spoken to two of the other people who may have potentially attended the initial workshop of the *Art4Fun* artists. Lionel Grange was there with Davina Hawkins. They'd only just met at the time of the workshops and Lionel remembers it as being rather uneventful. He didn't mention anything about the later workshops taking on a more experimental turn, and he couldn't recall if Davina's attitude towards the group changed at all during that time.

"Jackie Cayman didn't notice any change in Taylor Jenkins either," Whitton told Smith in the canteen.

She and DC King had paid Jackie a visit at her veterinary practice. Jackie and Taylor were in a relationship during the time of the workshops – she hadn't taken her up on the offer of attending the first one, and nothing struck her as odd about her while they were going on.

"That takes us back to square one," Smith said. "Those workshops are the key to this, but none of the people who took part can think of anything that might have happened during the course of them that could result in four women getting murdered."

"We've still got Patti Apple," Whitton said. "Bridge and Harry are there now."

"I need to talk to Samantha Rowland again," Smith said. "Those workshops need to be our main priority and she was the one who headed them up. It feels to me like we've been looking in all the wrong places. Perhaps it's not someone at the workshops themselves we should be searching for, but someone in the background. Where were these things held? Who else was aware of them?"

"I agree," Whitton said. "It's possible."

"I think the boss is losing it a bit," Smith said.

"We're all a bit on edge," Whitton said.

"He bummed a smoke off me earlier – DI Smyth hardly ever smokes, and he even suggested that Henry Harvey is still a suspect."

"He was in hospital when Taylor Jenkins was killed."

"I reminded him about that, but he reckons it's possible he could have slipped out of the hospital, killed Taylor and snuck back in without anybody realising. The bloke has a sprained ankle for Pete's sake."

"Does he though?" Whitton said.

"The doctor told us about it. He sprained his ankle and broke some ribs in the hit and run."

"The doctor only mentioned the broken ribs," Whitton said. "It was Henry who told us about the ankle."

"Are you sure?"

"Positive. I specifically remember the doctor only telling us about the broken ribs."

"It's still a bit farfetched to think he would do a runner from hospital to go out and murder someone."

"We need to make absolutely sure he was in hospital the whole time."

"I'll ask Baldwin to see if she can find someone to confirm it."

"What else did the artist tell you?" Whitton said.

"She's convinced the person who painted Jennifer Cole was emotionally involved with her," Smith said. "That painting stood out from the others in the emotion displayed in the brush strokes. Samantha Rowland thought the rest of the paintings were pretty cold by comparison. Clinical, she said."

"So, we should be focusing on Jennifer."

"She was the first victim," Smith said. "And the painting at the scene of her murder was very intricate. It will have taken a long time to complete. The background was done long before Jennifer was painted. *The Painter* made sure this one was perfect. Why is that?"

"It's obvious he's been planning this for some time."

"If we consider the timeline of the workshops," Smith said. "And if we assume they're the catalyst for the murders, it means he's had three years to prepare."

"All four were carried out with absolute precision," Whitton said. "Jennifer Cole and Paula Burton were lured with the advert for portrait painting. Davina Hawkins was surprised at home by someone posing as a courier, and Taylor Jenkins was attacked during her lunch break. But there's something I'm struggling to comprehend."

"There are many things I'm finding hard to understand with this one," Smith said.

"Even though he's put a lot of thought into the planning stages," Whitton said. "There are still far too many variables beyond his control. Take Davina Hawkins for example. If her fiancé hadn't stopped at the travel agents, he would have caught *The Painter* in the act. There is no way he could have predicted that the sous chef would forget to order the pastry. And look at Taylor Jenkins' murder. How could he know with a hundred percent certainty that Taylor would be alone in the shop during lunch hour?"

"He's been watching them," Smith said. "He's been keeping an eye on them for a long time. He knows their routines, and he knows the likelihood of those routines changing are slim."

"It still could have all gone wrong. What if Davina Hawkins had put up more of a fight? What if someone had been passing by when he forced his way inside her house?"

"Davina didn't put up more of a fight," Smith said. "And there was nobody around."

"But there could have been. I'm just saying that there are many ways that this could have gone wrong."

"There always will be," Smith said. "It is virtually impossible to devise the perfect murder. I don't even know if such a thing exists, but *The Painter* doesn't care. For him the risks are worth it. He is driven and his focus is on the killing and the subsequent paintings. I don't believe Davina Hawkins' fiancé could have changed the outcome if he'd caught them in the act. I get the impression that if he hadn't stopped off at the travel agents, he would also be dead."

CHAPTER FORTY SEVEN

Patti Apple looked like she hadn't slept in days. The skin on her face was sickly grey – her eyes were rimmed with red, and her lips were cracked. Her movements were sluggish, and Bridge wondered if she'd taken some kind of sedative. He and DC Moore were sitting with Patti in the kitchen of her house in Murton. The stench of the paint still lingered.

"I still haven't been inside the living room since it happened," Patti said. "I've tried but the closest I've managed to get was a hand on the door. I don't know if I'll ever be able to go back in there again."

"We're sorry to intrude," Bridge said. "But we'd really like to ask you a few more questions. We'll try to keep it brief."

"Are you feeling alright?" DC Moore said. "You look a bit peaky."

"I haven't been sleeping," Patti said. "Every time I close my eyes I see Jennifer in the chair. And the smell of paint won't go away."

"Is there somewhere else you could stay for a while?" Bridge said. "You mentioned a brother."

"Pete has his own problems. He has a hectic life with the business and his family, and I don't want to impose."

"What about friends?" DC Moore said.

"I can't run forever," Patti said. "I'm going to have to face what happened eventually."

"We'd like to talk about the *Art4Fun* workshops Jennifer attended," Bridge said. "If that's OK."

Patti nodded. "I suppose so."

"The workshops started in 2018," DC Moore said. "We've spoken to the woman who ran them, and she mentioned something about the partners of the artists being invited to the first one."

"Did you go?" Bridge said.

"I did," Patti said. "I didn't want to, but Jennifer could be very persuasive."

"Can you tell us about it," Bridge said.

"There isn't much to tell. It was a group of people getting together for a few drinks."

"Did Jennifer get on with these people?"

"I suppose so."

"Did you speak to any of them?" DC Moore said.

"Probably. Would you mind if I used the bathroom?"

"Of course not," Bridge said.

Patti stood up and shuffled out of the room.

"This is a waste of time," DC Moore decided. "She's like a zombie. She's in a real state."

"We need to find out more about those workshops," Bridge said.

"And I don't think Patti Apple is going to be able to help us."

"It's odd that you can still smell the paint. I would have thought it would have disappeared by now."

"Oil based paint tends to linger for ages."

"Hasn't she heard of air freshener?" Bridge wondered.

Patti came back inside the kitchen. A drop of water dripped from her chin.

"Sorry about that. I needed to splash some water on my face. I was prescribed some strong sedatives and the doctor said I may experience hot flushes."

"We were talking about the *Art4Fun* workshops," Bridge said. "You attended the first one. Did you go to any of the others?"

"I wasn't invited," Patti said.

"But Jennifer went to the rest of them?" DC Moore said.

"That's right."

"Do you know what happened at those ones?" Bridge said. "Did Jennifer talk about them?"

"She seemed to thoroughly enjoy them," Patti said. "She was really upbeat about them. And she said her art came on in leaps and bounds."

"Did the members of the group paint at the workshops?" DC Moore said.

"They did."

"Do you perhaps have any of the paintings Jennifer painted during that time?" Bridge asked.

"Probably."

"Would it be possible to see them?"

"What for? Why are you actually asking about the workshops? Surely you can't think Jennifer was killed by someone who attended them."

A mobile phone plugged into a charger on the wall started to ring. Patti made no effort to answer it.

"I don't know if you've been keeping abreast of the news," Bridge said.

"I haven't been able to focus on anything since it happened," Patti said. "And the sedatives have made everything hazy. What's happened in the news?"

"Jennifer isn't the only woman to have been killed recently," Bridge told her. "Three other women have lost their lives."

"All of them attended the *Art4Fun* workshops," DC Moore said.

Patti's eyes suddenly came to life. "You can't be serious?"

"I'm afraid it's true," Bridge said. "So, you can understand why we need to ask you about the workshops. Can you remember if Jennifer changed at all at that time?"

"Changed?" Patti said. "What do you mean, changed?"

"Did she start behaving differently?" DC Moore said.

"Of course not. She was enthusiastic about the workshops."

"Did she get on with the other members of the group?" Bridge said.

"I suppose so," Patti said. "She never moaned about any of them."

The phone started to ring again.

"Aren't you going to answer that?" DC Moore asked her.

"They can leave a message."

"You said Jennifer got on with the other people at the workshops," Bridge said. "Do you recall whether she became close to any of them in particular?"

"Close?" Patti repeated.

"It's not uncommon in things like that," Bridge said. "People tend to gravitate towards certain people. Did Jennifer ever mention anyone like that from the workshops?"

"She spoke of the other members rather vaguely if I remember. There wasn't one person she singled out."

"Do you know if she saw any of the members outside of the workshops?" DC Moore said. "Perhaps they met up for a drink or two."

"I would have known," Patti said. "Jennifer and I have been inseparable since we met. We're soulmates."

"Do you paint?" Bridge asked.

Patti's expression told him she wasn't expecting the question.

"No," she said. "I don't paint."

"Me neither," Bridge said. "I couldn't draw a stick man if my life depended on it."

"It doesn't mean I don't appreciate art though," Patti added.

"Would it be possible to take a look at some of Jennifer's paintings now?" Bridge said.

"I'd rather you didn't. It's very painful. You can't make me show you, can you?"

"No," Bridge said. "We can't. I understand. Can you at least talk about her art? What was Jennifer's preferred subject matter?"

"She used to dabble in all sorts," Patti said. "Landscapes, abstract, and sometimes she would experiment with different materials. Chalk on charcoal, for example."

"What about portraits?" DC Moore said. "Did she ever paint portraits?"

"Once or twice. I kept nagging her to do a self-portrait, but she insisted that she couldn't do it."

"Why is that? Bridge said.

Patti giggled. "Vanity. Jennifer always claimed that any artist who was reduced to painting himself was clearly a little bit in love with himself. She had some strange ideas sometimes."

"Just a few more questions," Bridge said. "And we'll leave you to get some rest. Going back to the initial workshop – did any of the other people there stick in your mind afterwards."

"For what reason?" Patti said.

"For any reason. Were any of them particularly memorable?"

"Most of them were rather subdued, even after a few drinks, although the loudmouth Cassanova did make quite an impression for all the wrong reasons."

"You're talking about Henry Harvey?" Bridge guessed.

"Henry," Patti said. "That was his name. There is nothing more repulsive than a good-looking man who knows all about it. It really is an unattractive trait in a person. That's one of the things I loved about Jennifer – she was naturally beautiful, and she didn't even realise it."

"You didn't make friends with Mr Harvey then?" DC Moore said.

"I was on guard the moment we were introduced."

"On guard?" Bridge said.

"I know a predator when I see one," Patti said. "And Henry Harvey was a predator of the vilest kind. And he was relentless."

"In what way?" DC Moore said.

"Jennifer made it quite clear about her preferences," Patti said. "She introduced me as her girlfriend, but Henry remained undeterred."

"Are you saying he still tried it on with her?" DC Moore said.

"More than once. You think what happened to Jennifer is linked to those workshops somehow, don't you?"

"We're looking into that possibility," Bridge replied.

"Then I would look more closely at Henry Harvey if I were in your shoes. There is something very wrong with that man."

CHAPTER FORTY EIGHT

"Henry?" Samantha Rowland said. "He was harmless."
Smith and Whitton had gone to see the artist at her house in Heworth. Smith had promised to make the visit a brief one. Bridge had outlined Patti Apple's concerns about Henry Harvey, and Smith wanted to see if the woman who'd headed up the *Art4Fun* workshops could shed any light on what Patti had told them. Henry Harvey had been involved in the hit and run, but the doctor who Baldwin had spoken to at the hospital couldn't swear that he was there the whole time. It would have been possible for him to have slipped out for a while without anyone realising. The doctor also confirmed that the only injuries Henry sustained were three broken ribs. He hadn't sprained his ankle in the accident.

"We believe he came on a bit strong with some of the women at the workshops," Smith said.
"And he was soon knocked down a peg or two," Samantha said. "I got the impression that Henry was the kind of man for whom rejection barely registered. Thick skin. Those types just shrug it off and move on to the next challenge."
"Did he strike you as someone who might become aggressive if he didn't get what he wanted?" Whitton asked.
Samantha laughed at this. "Not at all. Like I said, he was harmless. He was a good-looking man if I recall, and I doubt he has a hard time picking up a certain kind of woman."
"When we spoke earlier," Smith said. "We hit on the workshops, but we didn't really discuss them in much detail. The partners of the artists were invited to the first one, but only that one – is that correct?"
"It is. I know from experience how distracting the loved ones of an artist can be."

"Can you tell us about the workshops?" Whitton said. "What happened at them?"

"I like to give my students free rein," Samantha said. "Artistic license, I suppose you could call it, and I allowed them the choice of both subject matter and painting materials."

"Could you explain how that works?" Smith said. "Forgive me my ignorance, but what I know about art can be written on the back of a beermat."

"All the students would bring their own materials to the workshops. They were also responsible for whatever it was they wanted to paint. For instance I remember Henry brought along a single apple to the second workshop."

"What was your role in all of this?" Whitton asked.

"I was there to offer guidance. Nothing more. I made suggestions and observed the progress made."

"Did any of the students impress you?" Smith said.

"They were all talented in their own way," Samantha said.

"Even Henry Harvey?"

Samantha laughed again. "Even Henry. But if I have to think back, I'd say it was only Jennifer who demonstrated the flair of a real artist."

"What did she paint?" Whitton said. "Did she bring something with her to paint?"

"No. Jennifer was one of those rare artists who recreated from memory. She had an exceptional eye for detail. She probably would have made a very good detective."

Smith nodded. "Can you remember what she painted?"

"Not off hand, no," Samantha said.

"Are there any records of what the artists worked on?" Whitton said. "Photographs perhaps?"

"Not that I recall."

Smith's phone started to ring. The opening bars of Thomas Dolby's *You blinded me with science* told him it was Grant Webber. He rejected the call and made a mental note to get back to the Head of Forensics when they were finished talking to Samantha Rowland.

"Do you know if any of the students were close?" he asked her.

"I would say so, yes. Bonds were formed."

"Is that usual at these things?" Whitton said.

"It is," Samantha confirmed. "The creation of art is a very personal thing, and when you have a group of people involved in that creation process relationships tend to blossom."

"Why did you stop holding the workshops?" Smith asked.

"I believed they'd run their course. There was nothing more to be gained from them."

"The artists couldn't learn any more from you?" Whitton said.

"They weren't prepared to learn any more. As the old saying goes, you can take a horse to water…"

"What happened?" Smith said. "What changed?"

"The motivation for attending the workshops changed," Samantha explained. "I sensed the students were no longer there for the creative process. Attraction and jealousy began to muddy that process and I felt there was no point in carrying on."

"Do you know if any of your students formed relationships?" Smith said.

"I got the impression that that was the case."

"Can you tell us about anyone in particular?" Whitton said.

"Jennifer and Taylor. There was definitely a spark of something between Jennifer and Taylor."

"Even though both of them were in relationships at the time?" Smith said.

"You say that like it's never happened before."

"Fair enough. We'll let you get on."

"Thank you for agreeing to speak to us," Whitton said.

They both got to their feet. Smith shook Samantha's hand and thanked her again.

"Can I ask you one last question?" he said.

"Of course," Samantha said.

"In your opinion, do you believe any of the students who attended the workshops could be capable of murder?"

"You of all people ought to know that anyone is capable of murder if they're pushed hard enough."

Smith nodded. "You're not wrong there."

CHAPTER FORTY NINE

Smith got out of the taxi and walked up to the entrance of the Hog's Head. He'd agreed to meet Grant Webber for a drink and a bite to eat at the pub. That was the reason Webber had called him earlier. Whitton had declined. She didn't feel like going out, and Sheila Rogers had asked her to keep her company tonight.

Webber was sitting at the bar when Smith went inside the pub. A full pint of beer stood on the counter in front of him, and he was staring at something next to it.
Smith walked up to him. "What's that? New friend?"
He pointed to the black piece of rock on the bar counter.
"It's Obsidian," Webber told him.
"Now I'm getting worried," Smith said. "Not only have you made friends with a chunk of rock, you've given it a name too."
"It's a piece of Obsidian, you idiot. It's a healing crystal. I got it from Energy Emporium."
"You stole it?"
"Of course I didn't steal it. I saw it lying there and it piqued my interest. It's supposed to have healing properties. The label claimed it can help with emotional healing and letting go. I paid a pound over the asking price."
"Don't tell me you believe in all that stuff," Smith said. "I thought you were a man of science."
"I'm slowly coming to the conclusion that there is more to our existence than science can explain."
"I need a drink," Smith said. "I think it's going to be one of those nights."

He ordered a pint of Theakston and they sat down at one of the tables. Smith debated about what to have to eat, and in the end he settled on a steak and ale pie. Old habits were hard to break.

Smith held up his beer. "Cheers."

Webber obliged with his own beer. "What are we drinking to?"

"Healing crystals," Smith said. "And anything else you can think of."

"Billie suggested I take a step back from this one," Webber said out of the blue.

"Nobody would blame you if you did," Smith told him.

"Right. I thought I could handle it. I thought I could put some distance between the evidence and the memories that evidence has triggered."

"You're only human, Webber," Smith said. "And I never thought I'd ever say that about you."

"But this one isn't the same, is it?"

"What do you mean?"

"He doesn't use their blood," Webber said. "OK, he did with the first victim, but he doesn't use it exclusively."

"What else did you find at Energy Emporium," Smith changed the subject. "Apart from a piece of rock called Obsidian?"

"Nothing," Webber said. "I really don't know what I was hoping to see there. Whatever forensic evidence there was inside that shop, Billie will have found it. Are you going to catch this one?"

Smith took a long drink of his beer. "I really don't know."

"There's always a first time for everything."

"I can't afford to think like that," Smith said. "Whitton and me were discussing it earlier and even though it looks like he's planned for every possible eventuality, there are still a lot of things he had no control over. But I don't think he cares."

"It's imperative that he finishes what he sets out to do?"

"I think it is, but I still don't know what it is that's driven him to do what he's doing."

"Your motive is eluding you?"

"And that tends to make me a bit annoyed," Smith said.

The food arrived and Smith was glad. It would give him an excuse not to talk for a while. Webber's frame of mind was concerning, and Smith wasn't sure what to do about it.

"I didn't know you were vegetarian." Smith pointed to Webber's veggie lasagne.

"I'm not. I happen to really like this dish. Don't you ever feel like trying something other than the steak and ale pie?"

"When a man is tired of Marge's steak and ale pies," Smith said. "He's tired of life."

"Very philosophical. Bon Appetite."

Twenty minutes later Smith put down his knife and fork and let out a contented sigh.

"God, I love those things."

Webber had left half of his lasagne untouched, but Smith didn't comment on it.

"I know you pride yourself on the certainty of your science," he said instead. "But I want you to put that aside for a moment and look at the murders from the perspective of the killer."

"I look at what the evidence tells me," Webber reminded him.

"I get that," Smith said. "Just humour me here."

Webber stroked the stubble on his chin. "OK. He wants these women dead, and he wants to get away with it."

"What makes you come to that conclusion?"

"Have you caught him?"

"No."

"There you go then," Webber said. "You don't have a single suspect."

"We've still got Henry Harvey," Smith argued.

"Do you think he's *The Painter*?"

"No," Smith admitted. "He doesn't fit in so many ways."

"I believe when the identity of this killer is revealed," Webber said. "You will not have seen it coming. Not in a million years."

"It's happened before."

"Not like this it hasn't. This madman who calls himself *The Painter* will be someone you haven't considered once during the course of the investigation."

"You're actually quite good at this," Smith said. "Have you ever thought about a change of career?"

"More than once over the course of the past week."

"Do you think he's finished?"

"I do," Webber said without hesitation. "The haste with which he's dispatched his victims suggests he wanted to get this done in a hurry. There have been no further victims and the absence of a painting at the scene of his last one makes me believe he's completed what he set out to do."

A waiter came to clear away the plates and Smith ordered another couple of Theakstons.

"Last one for me," Webber told him.

"It's still early," Smith said.

"I'm knackered, and I really need to get some sleep. Let's talk about a topic that's not so dark. How's life as a grandfather treating you?"

"It's not as bad as I thought," Smith said. "Andrew is a really chilled baby, and he seems to have taken a shine to me."

"The poor child. How is his mother?"

"Lucy?" Smith said. "Wise beyond her years. I sometimes wonder which one of us is the adult. She's constantly going on at me about my language around the baby. She's terrified the first word that comes out of his mouth is going to be, *fuck*."

"It wouldn't surprise me."

"Are you really alright?" Smith said.

"I am," Webber insisted. "I really am. I think my new friend is actually having a positive effect."

"New friend?"

Webber tapped the piece of Obsidian.

"Oh, right. Your rock. Laura had a dream about a talking rock once. She has the strangest dreams."

"I wonder who she inherited that from," Webber said. "And I do not have a talking rock. It's a piece of Obsidian, nothing more."

Webber insisted on paying the bill. Smith was glad – he didn't have any money on him anyway.

"This was fun," he said.

"No it wasn't," Webber said. "But thank you anyway."

"I'll think about what you said."

"What did I say?"

"You said when I find out who *The Painter* is, I won't have seen it coming in a million years. I'll give it some thought. I'll see you tomorrow."

"You certainly will," Webber said.

Smith watched him go. He walked like a man with the weight of the world on his shoulders. Smith didn't envy him – he was on his way back to an empty house. Smith realised that even though the Smith household had become rather crowded in the past year he wouldn't change it for the world. Better a home full of chaos than a place where silence reigns.

CHAPTER FIFTY

Smith slept well that night and he couldn't understand why. When he opened his eyes to see the sliver of sunshine shining through a gap in the curtain, he felt more rested than he had in days. Even the deadweight of Theakston on his feet hadn't managed to disrupt a good nights' sleep. Smith shifted the portly Bull Terrier to the side and got out of bed. Whitton was breathing deeply on her side of the bed. Smith left her where she was.

He made some coffee and took it outside to the back garden. The curtains were all closed in the windows of the house next door. Sheila Rogers was clearly not up yet. Smith lit a cigarette and sipped his coffee. Fred shuffled outside and made his way over to Smith. The grotesque Pug grunted a greeting then made his way to the end of the garden to do what he needed to do.

"Good morning to you too, dog," Smith said.

He watched as the bug-eyed canine squatted on the grass and his gaze fell on something on the fence next door. Something didn't look right. He walked over to get a better look and that's when he realised what was wrong. The top panel had been smashed to pieces. Smith wondered how that could have happened.

He went back towards the house and picked up his coffee. He noticed that the roses next door needed pruning. Sheila wasn't much of a gardener and Smith knew the old owner of the house would turn in his grave if he could see the state of his prized rose bushes now. He took pride in those roses. Smith had lost count of how many times he'd thrown his cigarette butts over the fence just to spite the man. He debated whether to do it once more for old time's sake but opted not to. Instead, he stubbed the cigarette out in the ashtray and headed back inside the house.

He caught sight of something in his peripheral vision when he was by the back door. He turned to see what it was and gasped. The glass in the upper pane of Sheila Rogers' back door was broken and the door was ajar. Smith dropped the coffee and the cup shattered on the ground. He ran into the kitchen and raced through the house, almost trampling a Bull Terrier to death in the process. He unlocked the front door and went outside. He tried Sheila's front door, but it was locked, so he hammered as hard as he could on the wood.

"Shelia," he screamed.

The door was opened shortly afterwards by an utterly bewildered-looking Sheila Rogers. Her daughter, Fran was standing behind her.

"Where's the fire?" she asked.

"Someone has smashed your back door window," Smith told her.

"What?"

"The glass in the back door is broken."

"I haven't been in the kitchen yet," Sheila said. "I was actually fast asleep when I heard you trying to knock the door down."

Smith went inside her house. He told her to wait with Fran while he checked to see if everything was alright in the kitchen. As soon as he opened the door he knew everything wasn't alright. All of the drawers inside the room had been opened. The contents of the fridge had been scattered all over the floor. Smith took out his phone and called the switchboard. A PC he didn't know informed him someone would be there as soon as possible.

There was more carnage in the living room. The television was still attached to the wall but the contents of the entertainment unit beneath it were gone. The cupboards on the sideboard were wide open and a there were a number of framed photographs on the carpet.

"Oh my God."

Sheila had come inside the living room.

"Come on," Smith said to her. "We don't want to touch anything. Come next door with me and I'll make you a cup of tea."

"They've taken Fran's Netflix box," Sheila said.

"It's OK," Smith said. "It could have been worse. I've called it in, and someone will be here shortly. They're going to want to talk to you, but we can do that next door."

"Who would do such a thing?" Sheila asked Whitton.

They were sitting inside Smith's kitchen. He was talking to someone in the back garden on his mobile phone.

"It was probably kids," Whitton said. "It looks like they didn't get away with much."

Even though it was technically a house burglary, Smith had pulled in a few favours and got someone from the forensics team there straight away. He didn't think the burglary was connected to *The Painter* investigation, but he couldn't afford to take any chances. It didn't appear that much had been stolen and Smith came to the same conclusion as Whitton – this wasn't linked to the ongoing murder investigation - it was nothing more than an opportunistic burglary.

Smith came inside the living room.

"How are you feeling?" he asked Sheila.

"Numb," she said. "I know it's only a burglary, but to think someone was inside my house while I was asleep. It's creeping me out."

"Did you not hear anything?" Whitton said.

"Nothing. I sleep like a log, and so does Fran."

"Someone from the forensics team is next door now," Smith said. "They're going to need yours and Fran's fingerprints."

"Fran will love that," Sheila said.

"They'll make it fun for her," Whitton said.

"I've got hold of someone to fix the back door," Smith said. "They said they'll be here within the hour. I would also suggest you get the locks changed. It's possible that whoever broke in took a key with them. Don't worry – we'll get the place cleaned up in no time."
"You're being so kind," Sheila said. "I don't know how to thank you."
"There's no need for that. I'm also going to speak to someone about getting some uniforms posted outside the house for a few days."
"I thought you said it wasn't justified."
"My husband can be quite persistent when he puts his mind to it," Whitton said.
"Do you think I'm in danger?" Sheila asked.
"Probably not," Smith assured her. "It looks like it was just an opportunistic thing, but I'm not taking any chances."

PC Simon Miller came inside the kitchen.
"Sorry to bother you. Your daughter let me in."
"What is it?" Smith said.
"I need you to come and take a look at this, Sarge."

Smith followed him out into the sunshine. They went inside Sheila Rogers' house and PC Miller led Smith out to the back garden.
"I was checking to see if there was anything by the fence," PC Miller said. "It looks like this is how they made their getaway, and sometimes they drop things in their haste to get away. I didn't expect that though."
He pointed to the mound of earth at the bottom of the wooden fence. It looked like it had been freshly dug. A shovel was lying face down on the ground next to it.

Smith crouched down and scooped away some of the dirt.
"What the hell."
It was the cables he spotted first. He used the bottom of his T-shirt to expose them further and that's when he realised, they were attached to

Fran's Netflix Smart Box. Whoever had broken into Sheila Rogers' house hadn't taken their swag away with them – it was buried in a hole less than ten metres from the house.

CHAPTER FIFTY ONE

As baffling as the break-in at Sheila Rogers' house was, Smith had more pressing matters to attend to. Everything that had been taken in the burglary was found in the hole in the back garden. The pane of glass in the back door had been replaced, the locks on the doors were changed, and the fence had been repaired. Smith had been granted his wish and Sheila would have extra security in place in the form of a uniformed officer parked outside the house all day and night. DI Smyth had been reluctant, but Smith had put forward a good argument. He stressed that it was possible that *The Painter* was responsible for the break in and it was also possible that he would be back.

DI Smyth looked at the faces of the men and women on the team. The events of the past few days had clearly taken it out of them. They all looked exhausted and dejected, and DI Smyth didn't have a clue about how to change that.

"We've run out of steam," he told them. "Nothing we've covered thus far has given us any idea about the identity of *The Painter*."

"Webber reckons it's someone we haven't even considered," Smith said. "He said when we do catch him it will be someone we didn't suspect in a million years."

"Very helpful," DC Moore said. "He didn't happen to throw a name into the mix while he was spouting his ambiguous twaddle?"

"That's enough," DI Smyth said. "I suggest we rethink our strategy."

"In what way?" Smith said.

"You tell me. All we have from a forensic perspective is the time, place and method used. What else is there?"

"Why is he doing this?" DC King said.

"Why indeed," DI Smyth said. "Smith?"

"I think we need to focus entirely on Jennifer Cole."

"Forget about the other three victims, you mean?" Bridge said.

"For the time being. The painting left at the scene of Jennifer's murder was nothing like the others. The expert I spoke to described it as being an extraordinary piece, full of emotion. That painting was created by someone who has deep feelings for Jennifer. Someone who loves her dearly."

"You don't kill someone you love," DC Moore said.

"It's not as uncommon as you might think," Smith argued.

The sound of his ringtone cut short the discussion. It was Webber. Smith answered it and put it on speakerphone. "Please tell us you've found something."

"I don't know yet," Webber said. "I think the fourth victim may have had a secret camera inside her shop."

"What makes you think that?" DI Smyth said.

"When I was at Energy Emporium yesterday, I wasn't really sure what I was looking for so I took a whole lot of random photographs of the inside of the shop. I think I got lucky with one of them. When I examined them just now, I spotted something odd on one of the African masks behind the counter. I wondered why the masks had a *not for sale* sign on them and now I think I know why. Something in the mouth of one of them made me look twice. The flash of my camera was reflected in the mouth, and I wondered how that was possible. The mouth is just a hole, nothing else. It looks like the flash was reflected in the lens of another camera."

"I'll get someone to go and check," DI Smyth said. "Can you describe the mask in question?"

"I'll send you a photo of it," Webber told him.

"You say the mask is above the counter?" Smith said.

"That's correct."

"If there is a hidden camera in there, it'll have got the murder of Taylor Jenkins on tape."

* * *

It was confirmed thirty minutes later. Webber hadn't been seeing things – there was a tiny camera hidden inside the mouth of one of the African masks. All they had to do was find a way to retrieve the footage. It was possible the CCTV footage was linked to an app on Taylor's phone but that was going to take time to check. The phone was fingerprint protected, and it was quite a process to access the information on it without that fingerprint.

A search of Taylor's house had yielded a laptop, and it was also possible the footage from the hidden camera was on there somewhere. That was where the IT experts decided to look first. It was easier to bypass the security settings on a laptop. It was still going to take time though. DI Smyth had informed the team that they were probably looking at five or six hours at least.

"Why didn't the assistant tell us about the camera?" Bridge wondered.
"She didn't know about it," DC Moore said. "When we spoke to her, she said Taylor was paranoid about stuff going missing from the shop. I don't think anyone knew about the camera besides Taylor."
"What is it that takes the tech team so long?" Smith said. "I thought they just had to remove the laptop's hard drive and copy it into a program they have to retrieve the information on that hard drive."
"It's a bit more complicated than that where CCTV is concerned," DC Moore explained. "It depends on what system the footage is linked to. If it's something like *HiLook* it'll also be password protected, and they'll need to look into who provides the service. Best case scenario is the CCTV operators will hand over anything we ask them for."
"What's the worst-case scenario?" Smith said.

"They'll demand a warrant. As far as I'm aware they're not legally obliged to give us access to that kind of thing."

"It's time that particular law was changed then," Smith said.

"It is what it is," DI Smyth said.

The door to the small conference room opened and Baldwin came in. She was holding a package in her hands.

"What have you got there?" Smith asked her.

"It was just delivered to the front desk," Baldwin said. "It's addressed to you and the note on the front says it's urgent."

Smith took one look at the package and his heart stopped beating for a few seconds. It was wrapped in brown paper, but the shape and size left little doubt as to what it was.

"Fuck."

"Aren't you going to open it?" DC Moore said.

"Does anyone have a pair of gloves?" Smith asked.

He looked across at PC Griffin. He knew if anyone could help him it would be the beak-nosed PC.

He wasn't mistaken. PC Griffin took out a pair and handed them to him. Smith's hands were shaking as he started to tear open the brown paper. He managed to get half of it off and he gasped.

"It's Taylor Jenkins."

He removed the rest of the packaging to reveal the scene inside Energy Emporium.

The display of healing crystals was depicted in quite some detail. Smith knew that Webber's Obsidian was somewhere on the canvas. Taylor had been painted exactly as she'd been found. The only difference was the horns on her head and the reptile's tail sprouting from behind her. *The Painter* had taken great care with this painting, that much was clear. What was also quite apparent were the set of numbers right at the top of the piece.

"More GPS coordinates?" DI Smyth guessed.

"The bastard didn't even bother to disguise them this time," Smith said.

"He's made it easy for us."

"Harry," DI Smyth said. "Will you do the honours?"

"Already done, sir," DC Moore said.

"Well?" Smith said.

"This can't be right."

"Where is it?" Whitton asked.

"It must be some kind of mistake," DC Moore said.

"Where is it, Harry?" Smith said.

"16 Greenway Avenue."

Smith looked at Whitton and shook his head.

"He probably made a mistake," DC Moore said.

16 Greenway Avenue was very familiar to Smith. It ought to be – it was the house he'd lived in for more than twenty years.

CHAPTER FIFTY TWO

Lucy stepped away from the painting and smiled. She'd just finished the latest painting-by-numbers project and she was extremely pleased with it. This one depicted a beach scene, and the golden sky and azure beach were exactly how Lucy hoped they would turn out to be.

She was alone in the house. Darren had taken Andrew for a walk down to the park and Laura and Fran Rogers had gone with him. Lucy left the bedroom and went downstairs to get a glass of water. Theakston and Fred were nowhere to be seen and Lucy assumed they'd begged to go out for a walk too. She filled a glass with water and drank half of it in one go. Her phone started to ring on the counter. She walked over to see who it was and stopped dead. A noise close by caught her attention. It sounded like something had crashed to the ground. The phone stopped ringing.

Lucy wondered if Darren and his entourage were back. Was that what she had heard? She left the kitchen and walked up to the front door. She opened it wide but there was nobody there. The policeman in the car parked outside gave her a wave and she waved back. He'd been there all morning and Lucy felt sorry for him. She walked over and the window was wound down.

"Did you hear that crashing sound?" she said.

"I didn't hear anything."

"Would you like something to drink? I can make you some coffee."

"No thanks," the PC said and held up a flask. "I brought my own."

Lucy went back inside the house and closed the door behind her. She wondered if she'd imagined the mystery sound. She picked up her phone and saw she'd missed a call from Whitton. She was about to return the call when the front door burst open.

It was the policeman from the car.

"What's wrong?" Lucy asked him.

"I was told to get you out."

"What?" Lucy couldn't believe what she was hearing.

"DS Smith called and said I was to get you all out of here."

"I'm here alone," Lucy told him. "The others have gone down to the park. What's going on?"

"Come on," he held out his hand. "You can sit in the car."

Smith and Whitton arrived soon afterwards. Smith was out of the car before it even came to a complete stop. He ran towards his house and stopped when Lucy and the young PC got out of the police car.

"Are you alright?" Smith asked Lucy.

"I'm fine," she said. "What's happening?"

"Where's Laura?"

"Relax. She and Fran went with Darren and Andrew to the park. Are you going to tell me what's going on?"

More vehicles arrived on the street. Bridge's Toyota parked behind Whitton's car and he and DC Moore got out. DI Smyth was close behind them and another police car brought up the rear. Smith made a beeline for DI Smyth.

"False alarm, boss," he said. "I think he's fucking with my head."

"Why would he do that?" DI Smyth asked.

"Because he thinks he's in charge. I don't know."

"I want you to take your family and go and stay somewhere else for a while."

"What for?" Smith asked.

"Because we have to take this seriously. The GPS coordinates on that painting are a direct threat to you and your family."

"I'm not scared of this maniac," Smith said.

"Then you're a bigger fool than I thought. You need to get away for a few days."

"Not going to happen, boss."

Smith took out his cigarettes and lit one. He walked away from DI Smyth and looked up and down the street. The two uniformed officers in the second police car looked apprehensive. Smith got the impression they weren't entirely sure what their role in this was and he didn't blame them. Nothing was happening on the street. If *The Painter* had set out to cause confusion, he'd succeeded. A crowd of people had gathered to see what all the commotion was about.

He walked over to Whitton and Lucy.

"You said Darren took Andrew and the girls to the park," he said to Lucy.

"That's right," she said. "Mrs Rogers was grateful. She wanted to start tidying up the house and she said Fran would only get under her feet. The forensics officer left quite a mess in there."

"It can't be helped," Smith said.

"At least they found the stuff that had been stolen," Lucy said.

Smith looked at the house he'd spent the past two decades of his life in and something occurred to him.

"Where is she?"

"Where is who?" Whitton said.

"Sheila," Smith said. "Why hasn't she come out to see what all the commotion is about."

"Perhaps she hasn't noticed."

"No," Smith said. "Half of the neighbours are outside. You'd have to be deaf and blind not to notice all the action on the street."

A dog barked and when Smith turned to look, he saw it was Theakston. His faithful Bull Terrier had spotted him.

Smith walked back over to DI Smyth. "How accurate are GPS coordinates?"

"What?"

"GPS coordinates," Smith said. "Surely, they can't be used to pinpoint a single property. My neighbour hasn't come out to see what's happening. She was part of the *Art4Fun* group."

He ran up to Sheila Rogers' house and tried the door handle. The door was locked.

"Somebody get this door open," he screamed to nobody in particular.

PC Miller came over. "What's wrong, Sarge."

"Get this door open now."

It took three well-aimed kicks but on the third one the lock broke and the door swung open.

Ignoring every protocol he'd ever been taught Smith ran inside the house.

"Sheila," he shouted.

She didn't reply. Smith checked the living room. There was no indication that a crime had recently taken place in there. The room was spotless. Fran's Netflix box had been put back where it belonged. Sheila Rogers wasn't there.

"Sheila," Smith shouted again.

She wasn't inside the kitchen either, so Smith went upstairs.

He emerged from the house two minutes later. Darren, Andrew and the girls were standing with Whitton and Lucy. Fran started to walk in the direction of her house. Smith stepped forward and stopped her.

"I want to tell Mum about the ducks," she said.

"Not now, sweetheart," Smith said.

"She'll want to know about them."

"Not now," Smith repeated.

He glanced across at Whitton, lowered his eyes and shook his head.

Lucy noticed it. Her mouth opened wide, and her eyes fell on Fran. It was clear that Laura's best friend couldn't understand why she wasn't allowed to tell her mother about the ducks in the park. Lucy walked up to her and put her arm around her shoulder.
"Come with me."
"Why can't I see my Mum? I want to see my Mum."
Whitton came over. She wrapped her arms around the little girl and burst into tears.

CHAPTER FIFTY THREE

"How did he do it?"
Smith had found Sheila Rogers in the main bedroom. She was face down on the bed, and Smith didn't need to turn her over to know she was dead. The amount of blood on the sheets around her made that unnecessary. A quick check of the house told him there was no sign of forced entry. The back door was still intact, and it was locked from the inside. There were no broken windows and nowhere inside the house was there any suggestion that a struggle took place. The front door was also locked from the inside.

Whitton had been allowed to take some time off. Smith was never going to forget the expression on Fran Rogers' face when she was told she couldn't tell her mother about the ducks in the park. Little Fran wasn't going to able to tell her Mum anything ever again.

"How did he fucking do it?"
"Calm down," DI Smyth said. "We need to think."
"What is this bastard?" Smith carried on. "Some kind of fucking ghost. All the doors were locked. None of the windows were open and none of them were broken. There was a police car outside the house for fuck's sake."
"Did you find a painting?" It was PC Griffin.
Smith glared at him. "What?"
"Was there a painting anywhere near the body?"
"I didn't check."
"Why not?"
"What did you say?"
Smith got to his feet.
DI Smyth placed a hand on PC Griffin's shoulder. "Could you see if the tech team have made any progress with Taylor Jenkins' laptop. Now, please."

PC Griffin was out of the room in a flash. Smith sat back down.

He rubbed his eyes. "How did he do it?"

The words were spoken in a voice no louder than a whisper.

"Webber is there now," DI Smyth said. "If anyone can shed any light on this mystery it's him."

"Who was stationed outside the house?" Bridge said.

"PC Lewis," DI Smyth said.

"Never heard of him."

"He's recently transferred from Bristol. He's an experienced officer."

"He didn't do a very good job of protecting Sheila Roberts, did he?" DC Moore chipped in.

"PC Lewis will be interviewed in due course," DI Smyth assured him. "But by all accounts, he did what he was briefed to do. He kept an eye on the house. Nobody came or went after the little girl left to go next door to Smith's house. The kids set off for the park, and nobody went anywhere near the house. PC Lewis even had the presence of mind to remind Mrs Rogers to lock the door. As far as I'm aware he is not at fault."

"What now?" Bridge asked. "How are we supposed to catch someone who operates like this? He murdered someone inside a locked house with a police guard outside."

"What about the back?" DC Moore said. "We didn't have anyone watching the back, did we? Perhaps he got in through the back."

"The door was locked, Harry," Smith told him. "And there was no sign of forced entry."

"It's possible he was the one who broke in earlier," DC King said. "He could have taken a key to the back door."

Smith shook his head. "The locks were changed. I made sure of it. Besides, the door was locked from the inside."

The room fell quiet. Everyone inside it was in a state of shock. Smith's next-door-neighbour had been killed, and nobody could figure out how the murder had been carried out. It was a locked room mystery of the most bizarre kind.

"When was the last time you saw Sheila?" Bridge was the first to speak.
"Just after Jim Peters left her house," Smith said. "He was very thorough. The PC was in position outside the house, and I had to get to work. That was about eleven this morning. Fran left with Laura, Darren and Andrew about lunchtime according to Lucy."
"We got the painting an hour later," DI Smyth said. "And you and Whitton went straight home."
"He must have killed her shortly after her daughter left," DC King worked out. "He killed her and managed to get out of a locked house in a little more than an hour. I'm baffled."
"You're not the only one, Kerry," Smith said.

"The courier that delivered the painting is a dead end," DI Smyth said. "It was booked in first thing this morning, and an extra fee was paid to ensure it was delivered at a specific time."
"He paid in cash," Smith guessed.
"That's correct."
"Who booked the package in?" DC Moore.
"None of the employees of the courier company remember the package in question. It's a busy operation and apparently the volume of parcels is huge."

PC Griffin came back into the room. He held something up for everyone to see.
"I come bearing gifts."
"What is it?" Smith asked.
"Hopefully it's footage of *The Painter*," PC Griffin said. "The IT team came up trumps."
"Harry," DI Smyth said. "Let's get this up on the big screen, shall we?"

As far as Smith was concerned, DC Moore was taking far too long. He'd fetched his laptop and now he was busy connecting it via Bluetooth to the screen at the back.

"Can't you hurry things up a bit?"

"I'm going as fast as I can," the man from London told him. "Here we go."

All eyes were on the screen. The camera hidden inside the African mask covered a wide angle of the shop. The footage was frozen on the display of healing crystals opposite the counter. It also picked up the shelves on either side.

"We know Taylor Jenkins was killed between noon and one on Sunday," DI Smyth said.

"I'm getting there, sir," DC Moore said.

It didn't take him long to find the right place on the tape. DC Moore started it at normal speed. The time at the bottom was 11:59.

At 12:01 there was movement on the screen.

"That's Taylor's assistant," DC Moore said. "She's going on lunch."

She exited the shot and the camera picked up Taylor's back as she headed for the storeroom. Nothing else happened for a few minutes and then a figure appeared at the side of the screen.

"You can't see his face," DC King said. "He's got his head lowered."

"Do you think he knew about the camera?" DC Moore said.

"No," Smith said. "I don't think anyone knew about that apart from Taylor."

Taylor Jenkins appeared on the screen soon afterwards. There was no sound on the footage, but it was clear that she was talking. The other person in the shop didn't turn to face her immediately, but when they did come face to face Taylor's reaction was quite clear.

"She knows him," Smith said. "There's recognition there on her face."

What happened next was deeply unsettling, but everybody carried on watching anyway. The first slash of the knife came from nowhere, and there was nothing Taylor could have done to prevent it. The second cut was equally quick, and Smith knew she was probably dead before she hit the floor.

"Turn around," he willed. "Turn around and face the camera, you bastard."

His wish was granted shortly afterwards. *The Painter* took a number of photographs of the scene and turned around and looked straight at the hidden camera.

"No," Smith said.

"Holy crap," Bridge added.

"Webber was right," Smith said. "He said it was someone we hadn't even considered."

He got to his feet.

"Where are you going?" DI Smyth said.

"Where do you think I'm going, boss?" Smith said. "I'm going to pick up *The Painter*."

CHAPTER FIFTY FOUR

"I'm sorry about earlier, Sarge."

PC Griffin was driving far too fast for Smith's liking. Every available officer was on the way to the house they believed belonged to *The Painter* and Smith had drawn the short straw. Whitton and her car were at home, and DI Smyth in his wisdom had told Smith he was to drive there with his nemesis. Smith made a mental note to make the DI pay for it somehow, later down the line.

"I was a bit insensitive," PC Griffin said. "I didn't think."

"Don't worry about it," Smith said. "Concentrate on the road."

"I know how to drive."

The speedometer told Smith they were travelling at almost eighty miles-per hour.

They arrived five minutes later, and they were the first ones there. Smith was relieved when the car came to a halt, and he was able to get out. They'd parked up the road from *The Painter's* house. DI Smyth had insisted they wait until reinforcements arrived. It felt like déjà vu to Smith. It was always reinforcements where DI Smyth was concerned.

Smith took out his cigarettes and lit one. "Full circle."

"Sarge?" PC Griffin said.

"We've come full circle. This is where it all started."

He exhaled a huge cloud of smoke.

"I'm not sure you're actually allowed to smoke on duty, Sarge."

Smith replied to this with another blast of smoke.

"She killed the person she loved more than anything else in the world," he said. "I knew this was all about love."

The person caught on the hidden camera in Energy Emporium was Patti

Apple. *The Painter* was a woman, and she was the girlfriend of the first victim.

Backup arrived and Smith waited with the rest of the team while they searched number 45 Highfield Avenue. The bigoted man across the road from the house was taking a keen interest in the proceedings. Smith thought back to the first time he was here. It seemed like a lifetime ago now. He tried to piece together everything that had happened, placing Patti Apple in the middle of it, but he still couldn't think of a single reason why she'd done this. What reason could she possibly have to kill five women who attended an art workshop three years ago?

The first officers came out of the house after five minutes had passed. There was no sign of Patti Apple and Smith knew instinctively that she wasn't home. *The Painter* was still out there somewhere, and Smith didn't have a clue where to look. He threw his cigarette butt on the ground and stood on it. He walked up to the front door of number 45. As far as he was aware the house wasn't a crime scene – scores of officers had already trampled around inside, so he didn't bother with a SOC suit.

"Did you find anything inside?" he asked one of the PCs.
It was PC Simon Miller.
"She has a studio upstairs, Sarge," PC Miller said. "It was locked but we broke down the door. It's full of paintings. We didn't touch any of them."
Smith couldn't care less if they did. The video footage from inside Energy Emporium was more than enough. They didn't need anything else to confirm that Patti Apple was *The Painter*.

Smith went inside the house and the smell of paint hit his nostrils immediately. This wasn't the lingering scent of the paint used on the portrait of Jennifer Cole – this was paint that had been applied very recently. He wanted to see what was inside Patti's studio, so he went straight upstairs. Billie Jones followed him up.

"I heard about your neighbour," she said. "I'm sorry."

"Thank you," Smith said. "I never expected this in a million years. Webber said this would happen."

"Did he?"

"We had a meal out last night," Smith said. "And Webber said that when the identity of *The Painter* was revealed, it would be someone we wouldn't have thought to consider in a million years. All the time we were looking for a man, it was actually a woman behind the murders."

"Where do you think she is?"

"I have no idea," Smith admitted.

He went inside Patti Apple's art studio. The thick curtains were closed, and the room was dark. Smith opened them wide and took in the room. A number of easels stood on the floor. Most of the artwork on them looked unfinished. Various painting materials were stacked on a large table against one of the walls. Pots of brushes and mixing palettes stood next to different coloured paints. There were finished paintings hung up on the walls.

"We should be able to prove that the paintings found at the murder scenes were painted with these materials," Billie said.

"We don't need that kind of proof," Smith said. "We've got the video of her killing Taylor Jenkins."

"Webber will want all this bagged anyway."

Smith left her to get on with it. He took a closer look at the paintings on the walls. There were landscapes and paintings of buildings with people rushing past. Smith had to admit they really were very good. Patti definitely had an eye for detail. All of them had her signature on the bottom – *PA*, written in cursive.

One of the paintings stood out from the rest. This one was nothing like the others. Smith's initial thought was it was some kind of depiction of hell. Fires were burning on the canvas and a group of people were entwined in a carnal embrace. Legs and arms were twisted together in impossible ways and all of the people in the painting were naked. It was a disturbing scene, but Smith found himself drawn to it. It was the faces of the women in the piece that caught his eye. He recognised all of them – he ought to, they were all members of the *Art4Fun* workshop, and they were all dead. Sheila Rogers was there, twisted in an unnatural pose with Taylor Jenkins. Jennifer Cole's lips were glued to Paula Burton's enormous breasts. Something occurred to Smith when his eyes fell on the scrawl at the bottom of the painting. This one wasn't created by Patti Apple. The initials in the bottom left-hand corner were *JC*.

Jennifer Cole painted this.

Smith got Billie's attention and showed her the painting.

"Jennifer Cole painted this one," he said. "I think this is what it's been all about."

"It's rather pornographic, don't you think?"

"I think Patti saw what Jennifer had painted and became deranged with jealousy."

"But this is just a portrayal of some kind of fantasy," Billie argued. "It doesn't mean she wanted to act it out in real life."

"Patti didn't see it that way. To her this is betrayal of the worst kind. She loved Jennifer deeply, and I think this pushed her over the edge."

"She's clearly not well."

"I've seen enough," Smith said. "We still need to find the woman."

Bridge and DC Moore were in the kitchen when Smith went downstairs.

"She's definitely not here," Bridge said. "Where do you think she's gone?"

"She's not at work," DC Moore said. "According to them she hasn't been at work since lunchtime on Thursday."

"Has the house been thoroughly searched?" Smith asked.

"Of course," Bridge said.

"They even checked in the cupboard under the stairs," DC Moore joked.

Smith looked right at him.

"What?" DC Moore said.

"The cupboard under the stairs. I've got one in my house, and Sheila Rogers has an identical one. I think *The Painter* is still inside the house next door to mine."

CHAPTER FIFTY FIVE

Smith had been informed that Webber had finished at Sheila Rogers' house. Her body had been taken away and the house had been locked up. A police cordon had been set up around the property, and it would be off-limits for some time. It had been confirmed – nobody had checked the cupboard under the stairs. Smith didn't blame anybody for this oversight – he didn't think to check in there either. Why would he? The idea that a murderer would stick around at the scene of the crime was so preposterous it wasn't something anyone would consider.

"When you think about it," PC Griffin said. "It's the only logical explanation. It clears up the locked room mystery."
"Slow down a bit," Smith said.
PC Griffin had just taken a corner at sixty miles per hour.
"I know what I'm doing, Sarge," he said.
"Where did you learn to drive like this?" Smith asked him.
The lights up ahead turned to amber and PC Griffin slammed his foot on the accelerator. The car sped through the lights and narrowly missed a car coming from the left.
"Idiot," PC Griffin said. "Don't the lights and the siren mean anything these days?"
"Where did you learn to drive like this?" Smith asked again.
"I did three advanced driving courses," PC Griffin said. "I'm actually qualified to instruct. I thought it might come in handy in the job."
"That doesn't make me feel any better. There really isn't any need to drive like a Formula One driver."
PC Griffin obliged by decreasing his speed slightly.

The only car parked outside number 18 Greenway Avenue was a solitary police car. Smith had informed DI Smyth of his suspicions and once again he'd been ordered to stand by until backup arrived, but Smith had no intention of doing that. He was confident that the two officers in the parked car and he and PC Griffin would be enough to overpower one woman. PC Griffin came to a stop behind the other patrol car and he and Smith got out.

Smith walked straight up to Sheila Rogers' front door. He noticed that Whitton's car wasn't parked outside his house, and he wondered where she'd gone. Smith opened the door and ripped away the police tape in the process. He went inside with PC Griffin right behind him. The first thing they checked was the small cupboard under the stairs. Smith didn't think Patti Apple was armed. The knife that had been used to kill Sheila Rogers was found next to the bed she was found on, and Smith didn't think she would have a weapon on her.

He yanked open the cupboard door and stepped back. PC Griffin had a torch, and he shone the beam inside. The cupboard was empty.
"Fuck it," Smith said. "I was sure she would be in here. We need to check the rest of the house anyway. It's possible she's hiding somewhere else now the cavalry have gone."
"She might have already left the house, Sarge," PC Griffin suggested.
"The forensic team only left an hour ago," Smith said. "And there's been a car parked outside the whole time. I reckon she would wait for it to get dark. You check upstairs."

He made his way to the kitchen and stopped dead. It was rather surreal being here without Sheila present. He wondered what was going to happen to the place now. He assumed the landlord would be even more keen to sell after this. His thoughts turned to Fran. The poor little girl had nobody left. Her father couldn't give a damn about her, and her mother was dead. Smith recalled the promise he'd made to Sheila, and he wondered if he would be able to keep it.

There was nowhere to hide in the kitchen. Smith looked inside the living room. He checked behind all of the chairs and he even looked behind the curtains to see if Patti Apple was lurking there. She wasn't. Smith wondered if he was wrong, and she'd somehow managed to get out as soon as she'd killed Sheila Rogers. It's possible she could have gone out the back and somehow locked the door behind her with the key still in the lock on the inside.

Smith had reached the bottom of the staircase when he heard PC Griffin.
"Sarge."
The tone of his voice told him straight away that something was wrong. Smith looked up and saw the beak-nosed PC halfway down the stairs. Patti Apple was standing behind him, holding a knife to his neck.
"She came out of nowhere," PC Griffin said.
Smith stepped towards the bottom step.
"Get out of the way," Patti said.

There was something in her eyes that Smith found deeply unsettling – a fire seemed to be burning there, and Smith instinctively knew she was going to be unpredictable.
"He doesn't have to get hurt if you get out of the way," Patti said.
"You're not going anywhere," Smith said. "It's over."
"I will slice his throat open if you don't let me go."
"Go ahead," Smith told her. "I don't particularly like him anyway."
PC Griffin's eyes grew larger than Smith had ever seen them before.
"Sarge?"
"She's bluffing," Smith said.
"Don't push me," Patti said.
She pressed the blade of the knife harder against PC Griffin and a trickle of blood ran down his neck.

"It's over, Patti," Smith said. "I know this sounds like a cliché, but the whole place is surrounded. An armed team is in place, and they have orders to shoot you as soon as you step out of the house. I want you to think about that. Is this really how Jennifer would have wanted things to end?"

He wasn't sure why he said that, but he was running out of options. There was no armed unit outside. That part was a lie. For once DI Smyth hadn't thought it was necessary.

Smith wasn't expecting what happened next. Patti started to laugh. The childish giggle was somewhat inappropriate given the current situation. The laughter stopped abruptly and the hand holding the knife dropped to her side. She fell back and landed on one of the stairs. The knife fell from her grip and PC Griffin kicked it down the stairs.

Patti was now sobbing with her head in her hands. PC Griffin raced down the stairs and headed outside.
He stopped in the doorway and turned around.
"How did you know she was bluffing?"
Smith shrugged his shoulders. "I didn't."
PC Griffin observed him with real fear in his eyes. He placed his hand on his neck, turned and walked out of the door.

"You'll be taken away soon," Smith told Patti.
She wasn't listening. Her sobs were louder now, and she kept repeating two words over and over.
"Help me."

CHAPTER FIFTY SIX

"It wasn't real, Patti."
Smith was exhausted. He'd just been forced to endure three hours of Patti Apple justifying what she'd done. It had been three days since she'd been found in Sheila Rogers' house, and she'd refused to speak in those three days. Smith was worried she would never talk again. But then she'd found her voice and agreed to be interviewed. Neither Smith nor DI Smyth were holding their breath when they started the interview. They didn't think she was going to tell them anything useful. They were both wrong.

She'd come across the painting purely by chance. She was off work with a bout of the flu and Jennifer had been at the school where she worked as a teaching assistant. The painting of the five women was hidden in the cupboard under the stairs. Patti hardly ever went in there, but a faulty element on the kettle had caused the mains to trip. The distribution board was located inside the cupboard, and Patti had gone to flip the switch back up. That was over a year ago. The carnal scene on the canvas had caused something to break inside her and Patti had been overcome with rage and jealousy.

The country was still in the grip of the pandemic at the time, and it would have been impossible to carry out what she had in mind with the lockdown in place, but it gave Patti plenty of time to plan. She spent hours figuring out how to make the women in the painting pay for the damage they'd done.

"It was a fantasy," Smith said. "A fantasy transferred to the canvas. It wasn't real."
Patti looked at him with wild eyes. "You don't know anything about art."
"I know a bit more than I did a week ago."
"You know nothing."
"I know a bit about cold-blooded killers though," Smith said. "I thought I'd

seen everything, but I've never come across anything like you. You murdered five women because of something that existed solely in the sick recesses of your mind. Jennifer didn't plan on re-enacting what was in the painting – that's the whole point of it. It was nothing more than a fantasy. She had no intention of betraying you in any way."

"That painting was much more than an expression of carnal desire," Patti said. "You'll never understand."

"There are some bits I'm still finding hard to comprehend," Smith said. "Would you be able to fill in the blanks for me?"

Patti rolled her eyes and nodded.

"For the benefit of the tape," DI Smyth said. "Miss Apple is nodding her head."

"We found some deleted messages on Jennifer's phone," Smith said. "Between her and someone who claimed to offer portrait painting. Was that you?"

"What do you think?" Patti said.

"What was the point of that?" DI Smyth said. "Why go to all the trouble when you had plenty of opportunities to kill her?"

"It was supposed to be a bit of fun. A surprise. I was the one who had the flyers printed. I left one on the table in the hallway, making sure Jennifer would see it. I'd prompted her for a while suggesting she get her portrait painted and she fell for it. When she opened the door and saw it was me, the look on her face was priceless. She got into the spirit of it though. I poured her some wine, and we got into our separate roles beautifully. It felt like a date night. Jennifer even told me the portrait was a gift for her girlfriend. I'd never been so in love with her than I was right then."

"Right before you killed her?" Smith reminded her.

"You wouldn't understand."

"Can we assume you used the same ruse on Paula Burton?" DI Smyth said.

Patti smiled at this. "I wasn't sure she would go for it, but she did. I knew the house on Norman Street was standing empty, so I lured her there. I didn't like her – her vanity was her downfall."

"Davina Hawkins put up a bit of a fight," Smith said. "You weren't expecting that, were you?"

"C'est la vie," Patti said. "I wasn't expecting her to recognise me, but she did. It didn't change anything, did it?"

"What about the courier van?" DI Smyth said. "You used a Harvey's Courier van in the first two murders. Why did you do that?"

"That was Henry's idea."

"Henry Harvey had nothing to do with any of it," Smith said.

"I didn't mean he was involved," Patti said. "At the first workshop Henry was a bit drunk. He was so full of himself – thought he was some bigshot entrepreneur with his courier business, and he was bragging about the fleet of vans. It gave me an idea. Courier vans are everywhere, and nobody pays them much attention. I went there one day, posing as a potential customer. Henry didn't even recognise me. That's when I saw the keys on the board behind the desk. The idiots even wrote the registration numbers on the keyrings. It was easy to steal a set and come back and borrow one of the vans."

Smith was starting to feel slightly ill. When Patti Apple had refused to speak, he'd been concerned that she wouldn't be deemed fit to stand trial but now he was absolutely convinced she would. What she'd confessed to today were the words of a calculated murderer. Every step had been planned carefully and even the most gifted defence lawyer wouldn't be able to convince a jury that Patti wasn't in control of her actions at all times. It was little consolation though. Patti Apple would no doubt spend the rest of her life in jail, but it wasn't going to change what she'd done. It wasn't going to bring Sheila Rogers back. Sheila was an innocent party in all of this, and now Fran was going to grow up without a mother. The little girl was too young to understand why she was never going to see her mum again, and Smith didn't have the words to explain it to her.

"I think we've got everything we need," DI Smyth said.
He looked at Smith for confirmation of this.
"Just one more thing," he said. "Why paint them? Why did you paint them after you'd killed them, and why did you leave clues about your next victim in the paintings?"
"It seemed like a fun thing to do," Patti said.
"Fun?"
"It kept you on your toes, didn't it?"
"How did you even get my email address?" Smith said. "That was my personal email address."
Patti smiled a smug smile. "Your wife gave it to me."
"No, she didn't."
"Oh but she did," Patti insisted. "She and the other female detective came to speak to me, and she gave me her card, only it was an old one of yours. She even said you wouldn't mind."
Smith remembered the old cards he'd had made. It was a long time ago, and Patti was right – his personal email had been on those cards.

DI Smyth indicated that the interview was over by stating the time for the tape and Smith got to his feet.
"What's going to happen to me?" Patti said.
Smith didn't bother replying. It was out of his hands now, and he really didn't feel like spending one more second in the room with Patti Apple.
"Your legal representative will explain that to you," DI Smyth told her. "But I wouldn't get your hopes up about seeing the outside of a prison cell again."

Smith left the room without even looking back. It was over but there was still a long road ahead. He had some decisions to make, and he needed time to think about them carefully before he decided on the best route to take.

CHAPTER FIFTY SEVEN

"There's no going back," Whitton said. "Once you sign that, that's it."
Smith looked at the piece of paper on the table in front of him. He closed his eyes and opened them again.
"Fuck it."
He picked up the pen and signed his name at the bottom next to where Whitton had signed hers.
"That's that then."

"Everything should run smoothly," Dawn Penny informed him. Dawn was the solicitor representing the sale of number 18 Greenway Avenue.
"The mortgage has been pre-approved, and the owner of the property is pushing for a quick sale," Dawn added. "Mrs Rogers' rent was paid up until the end of August so technically you should be able to move in anytime."

The purchase of the house Sheila Rogers rented had been the second most difficult decision Smith had had to make. The price had been reduced drastically for a quick sale, but the owner still hadn't had any bites. Properties where brutal murders had taken place weren't particularly well sought after, but Lucy and Darren told Smith it didn't bother them when Smith put forward his suggestion. They would have number 18 to themselves. Andrew would be able to have his own room, and they would have some privacy. It also meant the Smith household would be less crowded.

Especially now there was to be another member of that household. The decision to honour the promise made to Sheila Rogers had been the hardest one to make. Taking on any child was going to be a challenge but adopting the daughter of a murder victim increased that challenge tenfold. Smith knew that from experience, but Fran had nowhere else to go. Her father wasn't interested, and Smith had been told it was either him and Whitton or a foster family of strangers. Smith couldn't allow that to happen, and he and Whitton had set the ball rolling. It was by no means guaranteed that the adoption application would be successful, but the social worker they'd been dealing with had been optimistic. Fran would take over Lucy's room. Laura would have another sister in the house.

There was still a long way to go and Smith knew it wasn't going to be easy, but he could see no other way. It had been three weeks since Sheila Rogers had been murdered by *The Painter*, and Fran had barely spoken a word in that time, but Smith was confident she had the right people around her to help her get through the death of her mother. Lucy was right next door, and if anyone knew exactly what she was going through right now it was Lucy.

"No regrets?" Dawn asked.
"I'll let you know in six months," Smith told her.
Dawn raised an eyebrow.
"Don't pay any attention to my husband," Whitton said.
"I'd better be off," Dawn said and picked up the paperwork. "I'll get this submitted, and I'll email you copies of everything."
"Thanks," Smith said.
"I'll see you out," Whitton said.

Smith followed them. They said their goodbyes to Dawn Penny and watched her drive away. Smith looked at the house next door.
"I can't believe that's ours now."
"We're property moguls," Whitton said. "Who would have thought we'd ever own two properties. You have got to be kidding me."
She was staring at something further up the street. She turned to look at her husband.
"I've been meaning to tell you about that," Smith said.

"What have you gone and done?"

They watched as the red Ford Sierra approached and stopped outside the house. Darren Lewis got out and walked up to them. Darren had recently passed his driving test. He handed the keys to Smith.

"Are you going to let me know what's going on?" Whitton said.

Smith wasn't listening. He'd walked over to his old Sierra, and he was busy inspecting the paintwork. The car looked brand new.

Whitton and Darren joined him.

Darren handed Smith two sheets of paper. "Our Gary asked me to give you the invoice."

"It's paid for," Smith reminded him.

"I know," Darren said. "I thought you might want to keep it. Just about every component of that car had to be replaced. Gary said he's never done a job like it. He told me to tell you he knows a bloke who can help get it through the MOT if you have any problems."

"I'll pretend I didn't hear that," Smith said.

"I thought you said it was past saving," Whitton said.

"It cost me a bit," Smith told her.

"How much are we talking about?"

"That's not important," Smith said. "There are certain things in life that are worth saving, regardless of the cost. Shall we take her for a spin?"

THE END

Printed in Great Britain
by Amazon